Freedom's Just Another Word

Freedom's Just Another Word

CAROLINE STELLINGS

Second Story Press

Library and Archives Canada Cataloguing in Publication

Stellings, Caroline, 1961-, author
Freedom's just another word / by Caroline Stellings.

Issued in print and electronic formats.
ISBN 978-1-77260-011-7 (paperback).--
ISBN 978-1-77260-012-4 (epub)

I. Title.

PS8587.T4448F74 2016   jC813'.6   C2016-903533-6

C2016-903534-4

Edited by Kathryn Cole, Carolyn Jackson
Designed by Melissa Kaita
Cover photo © iStockphoto

Photo on page 202: June 26, 1970,
Winnipeg Free Press, reprinted with permission.

Printed and bound in Canada

*Second Story Press gratefully acknowledges the support of the
Ontario Arts Council and the Canada Council for the Arts for our
publishing program. We acknowledge the financial support of the
Government of Canada through the Canada Book Fund.*

Canada Council   Conseil des Arts
for the Arts   du Canada

Funded by the Government of Canada
Financé par le gouvernement du Canada

Published by
SECOND STORY PRESS
20 Maud Street, Suite 401
Toronto, ON M5V 2M5
www.secondstorypress.ca

For Olga and Sylvia–since 1970, my very best friends

PROLOGUE

You know your life must be seriously messed up when the one who straightens it out for you is Janis Joplin. Not that I don't have the utmost respect for the blues-rock singer—I do. Sure, she drank too much. She was drinking the heart right out of a summer afternoon the day I met her. And when I saw her again in Texas, she was so high on heroin, her eyes looked like two little television screens, reflecting a dead channel.

But when she sang—oh, when she sang—that tempered-in-a-forge voice of hers was like a flame in this burned-out world. You'd have to be stone-deaf or a cadaver not to be electrified by her; she could sound as smooth as the Southern Comfort that dribbled from the corners of her mouth, or as gritty as walking on spilled sugar. And the way she clutched every stanza like it was her last made me shake with anticipation.

It was an unwritten rule for musicians to be strung-out

back then. The 1960s were, after all, one big love-fest; an endless chain of events where stoned hippies sat in fields and listened to some of the best music that the world has ever produced and couldn't appreciate it because they didn't know where the hell they were. Monterey Pop, Woodstock, the Isle of Wight—it's a pity that these concerts went by in a purple haze because they will never be repeated. Never.

The year I met Janis Joplin—1970—was a turning point in many ways. It was the year that the Beatles stopped being the Beatles. The year that Jimi Hendrix died of an overdose in London, and Simon and Garfunkel recorded their last album together. It was the year that Janis took her final fix at the Landmark Motor Hotel. Booze, heroin, desperation—that's what killed her.

The end of a life is such a definite thing—no wiggle room whatsoever. But I don't think anyone's life really begins at birth. Being born is just a technicality. Everyone chooses a certain moment, a particular experience from which they look ahead, and to which they return, time and again, wondering if life would have been different had that one incident never occurred. For me, it was meeting Janis—Pearl, as she chose to be called—outside a liquor store in Saskatoon, Saskatchewan.

CHAPTER ONE

Every road in Saskatoon leads sooner or later to the South Saskatchewan River, that *grande dame* of a waterway that meanders through the center of town. She's stout, dark blue, and dependable. She glides past the upscale hotels and well-turned-out office buildings the same way she always has, keeping time like a watch and a careful check on the residents: the mothers herding their children, old people talking in low voices about how everything's changed, husbands waiting patiently in parked cars, and long-legged delivery boys staggering under loads of groceries.

The farther the citizens get from the river's vigilant eye, though, the more they are apt to drink and gamble, and if you drive far enough west on 20th Street, where gang graffiti appears on every surface marking territory like cat spray, you can see drug addicts shooting up and fourteen-year-old girls "walking the strolls." Some are white, some are Aboriginal; all of them are desperate. If they were black, you'd think you were in the south side of Chicago. Or Harlem.

Growing up in Saskatoon, I'd never seen a black hooker, mostly because there were so few blacks in Saskatoon to begin with. I'm black (well, half-black), but other than one old man at whom everyone pointed because his grandfather had been a slave, and a girl in school who wasn't allowed to come to my birthday party because we played music and kept Jesus out of the house, there weren't any black people in my neighborhood at all. Besides us.

I wasn't raised in the upscale area, but I didn't live in the gutter either. I lived with my parents, Clarence and Thelma Merritt, not far from downtown, on a street that had a few trees, and was safe enough that you could go out after dark without being armed. Clarence was a mechanic, and we lived over top of his garage. I didn't mind it as a child, but by the time 1970 rolled around, and I was eighteen, I'd spent many a night peering into that dark sinkhole known as my future, craftily planning how I'd get the hell out of Saskatoon.

Because the only things I could do with any degree of success were motor mechanics and singing the blues, I knew that if I didn't find a nightclub to take me on, I'd be changing oil and rotating tires for the rest of my life. There was only one genuine club in the city, Saskatoon Blues, but it was reserved for big names. They didn't hold auditions for amateurs. There was also a trashy kind of place near our garage called The Beehive; it was an octagonal building, with huge ceramic bees on the roof and hardly any customers below it, but the owner wouldn't let me sing there, anyway. He said I wasn't ready, but I knew the real reason was because I was the product of an affair that my father had with a white woman.

Her name was Wendy Wood and I'm sure she was a prostitute. Thelma never said so, but that's what I think. It was a cold night in February when she scaled the fence. My father found her sleeping in one of the cars on his lot, so he brought her inside. Gave her a bed. Gave her a meal. Gave her a home. She became pregnant with me the following summer, and after I was born, she turned me over to Clarence and Thelma. They never saw her again. They got one letter at Christmas, postmarked in Alberta. (She didn't ask about me.)

Then, when I was sixteen, a customer pulled up in a Studebaker Starlight coupe that needed a new muffler. He told us that a drunken woman outside a homeless shelter in downtown Calgary had grunted something to him about Clarence and his work with classic cars after he'd tossed her some change. We figured it was Wendy Wood.

Thelma never blamed Clarence for the affair, never took it out on me, never made me feel like a bastard child. She loved me as if I was her own. Clarence said it was because she'd always wanted to have a baby but never could. The rest of the neighborhood was shocked when it happened, and the older folks never got over it—a married black man impregnating a young white woman. It was worse than being born in the backseat of a bus. Eighteen years later, some people were still talking about it. Mrs. Hill—a dusty little woman who ran a boarding house next door and who (without knowing it) hollered *ah-screwyou* every time she sneezed—made sure nobody forgot. Like the river, she kept careful check on the entire community. She knew who drank, who smoked, and who slept with whom. And she disseminated the information through an espionage system that involved the local beauty parlor, the grocer, the shoe repair shop, and a tearoom that advertised palm reading in its foggy, limp-curtained window. She even coerced the mailman into letting her look at postcards; she said she liked to see the pretty pictures, but always managed to sneak a peek at the messages.

That was how she kept the Wendy Wood story going, and that was why so many people drove to the other side of town to have their cars fixed, and why I never got to sing at The Beehive, and why I hated Wendy Wood, and why I hated Saskatoon. I figured I'd go to Toronto, or better yet, back to Louisiana where my parents came from.

That's my name, Louisiana.

Easy for short.

And that's where I'd hoped to go one day, once I had enough money saved. I figured I might buy a real nice, classic car—the kind Clarence specialized in. Something really fine that would suit a blues singer. I wanted to make something of myself. I wasn't going to settle into marriage and kids, not me. That would have been like death. Once I'd gotten through the hell of high school, I noticed that my friends were starting to throw their lives away. I'm not talking about the ones I drank lemon gin with under the bridge—their lives were over by the ninth grade. I'm talking about the ones who were trying to get ahead by studying accounting through correspondence courses or enrolling in hairdressing school or learning shorthand. The path to nowhere. That's how I saw it. The bottom rung on the ladder to happiness.

So I stuck it out in the garage and saved every dime I earned. At least there I could listen to my parents' old blues records while I worked—Bessie Smith's "Lou'siana Low Down Blues" got me through many dull, rainy mornings replacing fan belts and scraping the corrosion off battery terminals.

Got a loaded feelin'
A loaded feelin' I can't lose my heavy load
Got a loaded feelin' I can't lose my heavy load
My home ain't up north, it's further down the road.

I'd always had a strong voice. Clarence and Thelma recognized it right away and encouraged me to sing even before I could talk. And Clarence taught me the *frottoir*. That's an instrument used in zydeco—the Cajun blues they play in Louisiana. The frottoir looks like a washboard, and you hang it around your neck, but it makes a great *scratchety-scratchety-scratchety* sound and keeps better time than a snare drum. Clarence played it every Saturday night. Thelma would make a big pot of gumbo, and we'd put on records by Clifton Chenier, King of the Bayou, and Thelma would get out her accordion and I would sing. It was loud and crazy and the most fun I'd ever had in my life. Sometimes we'd be real quiet and somber and listen to Billie Holiday sing "God Bless the Child." Thelma cried every time she heard that one. Even at five or six years of age, I did my best to sound as good as that. By the time I was ten, I could make Thelma cry too.

That was when she decided I should have proper voice lessons, and that was when Miss Poultice—the first racist I'd ever met—came into my life. There would be more to follow, but you know what they say about the first cut being the deepest.

A tall, skeletal woman, she always wore the same tan suit and mauve blouse when she taught piano, singing, and dancing in the parlor of her home on Clover Street. She told Thelma she had so many people trying to get a place with her that she could only squeeze me in on Thursday afternoons, but other than one piano student, a red-headed boy who lifted his hands about three feet off the keys and came down on the wrong notes, I never saw anyone else there on Thursdays.

Miss Poultice would walk the boy out the door, smiling all the while. She'd chat with his mother and tell her how well the kid was coming along. And then, with a tortured expression, she would sigh heavily as she put away his sheet music and got out mine. Not because I wasn't a good student, not because I couldn't sing, and not because I didn't want to learn.

She started each session with breathing exercises. "In through the nose, out through the mouth," she'd say, while poking the end of her pen into my rib cage. (She touched the boy with her bare hand, but not me.) Next she'd demand that I watch her diaphragm while she sang "Now is the Month of Maying," the song she was teaching me for a soon-to-be-held recital.

Now is the month of Maying,
when merry lads are playing,
fa la la *la la la* la *la* la
fa la la,
la la la,
la la la.

Miss Poultice didn't like me; I think that's why she gave me that song. I asked her please, couldn't I sing the blues; she was aghast and declared that *Negro music* had no place in her school. (Nor, I gathered, did Negroes themselves if she could find enough white students.) Then, during our last lesson, just a day before the recital, I had to use her bathroom and left the room. When the phone rang, I heard her tell the person on the other end that she'd call her back in a minute, once she was done with the *Negro* girl. The other person said something, then Miss Poultice replied, "Oh, don't you worry, I'll use Lysol."

I thought about telling Thelma and Clarence, but didn't want them to be upset, or feel guilty for taking me to Miss Poultice. Then I tried to dream up ways to get out of the stupid recital in her stupid stuffy parlor. Finally, I decided that the best way to stick it to Miss Poultice was to go ahead and sing at her recital.

Yeah, I told myself. *I'll make her wish she hadn't said that.*

The next evening, six sets of parents jammed themselves into chairs, all side by side in a semi-circle. Clarence and Thelma were the first to arrive, and could have sat right next to the piano, but living so many years in Louisiana, they'd trained themselves to leave the best seats for the white people. They found a place against the back wall.

First, a sweaty-fingered girl with thick glasses pulled herself in close to the piano, then, with lowered wrists and high knuckles, leaning forward and pressing heavily on the keys, she banged out "The Dance of the Forest Animals" with great big long waits between notes. Following her, an uninspired rendition of a barely recognizable tune by the red-headed boy led to the bored rattle of programs, nervous scraping of chairs, and, finally, polite soft applause with just the tips of the fingers.

The voice students were worse than the pianists. The first one, a chubby girl with wet spots under her arms, sang "How Much is that Doggie in the Window." She stuck out her lips and wrinkled her forehead and sang in a baby voice that would make you gag. The next, singing "Pixie in the Glen," had a voice so loud and so jarring it sounded like she was spilling marbles. At least it woke everyone up. Their wakeful state didn't last, however. The dancer who followed leapt around the tiny space between the piano and the parents in a pink tutu, and the leg that was supposed to be pointed at the ceiling hung down like a broken wing.

I was left until the end. Thelma and Clarence sat up in their chairs, and everyone looked at them, since it was obvious whose daughter I was. I cleared my throat and raised my chin, and as Miss Poultice moved the sheet music for "Now is the Month of Maying" to the piano, I held up my hand.

"Miss Poultice?" I asked earnestly.

"Yes?"

"If it's all right with you and with everyone here, I'd prefer to sing without the piano tonight."

Looking from side to side, and not knowing what to say when she saw the parents nodding their heads, Miss Poultice had no choice but to let me sing unaccompanied.

Figuring that "The Month of Maying" was too tame for a *Negro* girl, I opted instead for Bessie Smith's "Send Me to the 'Lectric Chair." I belted out the song, and when I got to the last verse, gave it everything I had:

I wanna take a journey,
To the devil down below,
I done killed my man,
I wanna reap just what I sowed.

That was the end of my lessons with Miss Poultice, but I learned something about being a blues singer. You have to be pissed off at somebody or something. That's what gives you the edge.

CHAPTER TWO

Thelma died when I was seventeen.

She'd been looking forward to my high-school graduation for as long as I could remember. We'd picked out my dress pattern several months in advance. She cut out the pieces on our big wood table that was made from a kind of knotty pine that grows down in the bayou, and was thick and chunky and sturdy, so you could stick pins in it and it wouldn't feel a thing. Clarence and Thelma brought it with them in their truck, all the way from Louisiana.

They brought an old Singer sewing machine as well. It was Thelma's mama's, and it still ran like new; Thelma made all her clothes with it. Clarence's overalls too. I wasn't one for dresses, but Thelma chose a style that was elegant, then found a beautiful dark green fabric that cost more than five dollars a yard at Woolworth's. And she bought me shoes and gloves to match. When I tried it all on, she sighed and said I looked like Diana Ross.

"Diana Ross?" I said. "C'mon, Thelma. She's not a blues singer."

"No, but she's attractive."

"I guess. But I don't like her music."

"I thought you liked Motown, Easy," she said, marking the hem length while I stood on a chair. "You told me you liked all types of music," she added through the pins in her mouth. "Anyway, in a dress, you look like her. So there."

I don't know why Thelma thought I was attractive. How could I be? I was a product of Wendy Wood, and she certainly wasn't. Thelma and Clarence had a couple of photos of her. I thought she was ugly. She even had teeth missing in the front.

Thelma was an optimist, I guess. And she was the kind of woman who, if you put her inside any four walls, however dismal, she could turn them into a home. According to real estate standards, ours was a modest dwelling, but when I came home every day from school to the smell of bread baking and soup boiling and spray starch and scorch from Thelma's iron, our little place over the garage was the warmest place on earth.

While Thelma pinned up the hem, I asked her about life in the bayou.

"Who needed money?" was her response when I asked about being poor. "We had music, and we had food. That's all anybody needs." It was a good thing she felt that way, because after her daddy died at a young age, her mama got hitched to a real crook of a man. He was a gambler with yellow eyes who rode up and down the river on a paddle-wheel boat and lost every dime they had.

"Mama was glad I found a good man like Clarence," Thelma told me. "She died happy, knowing I was looked after."

Why does she always tell me that Clarence is a good man? Is she trying to convince herself? Or me?

The dress turned out great, but I never made it to my graduation after all. I wouldn't go without Thelma. I put it away in a box in my closet and didn't dare look at it, because I knew that the sight of those stitches would mean I'd be hit with a wave of unbearable pain.

Clarence didn't cry when Thelma died, but after that day, he never smiled once. He just went about his work, answered any questions his customers had with a nod of the head or as simple an explanation as he could muster. Even with me, he used as few words as possible. He let me listen to blues records, but never joined in. Not without Thelma. I still played the frottoir and the accordion, but not at home; I used them to busk outside the liquor store for extra cash.

Every night before bed Clarence stared at Thelma's picture. It sat over the fireplace. I thought he was talking to her in his head, but nothing came out of his mouth and his lips didn't move. There was something in his eyes, though; a sort of faraway look that told me he was thinking about her and remembering what it was like back in the bayou, when they were young. I wondered if he still felt bad about what happened with Wendy Wood. I wondered if, when he looked at me, it reminded him.

I hoped not.

I hoped not because other than Thelma, Clarence had led a crappy life.

Thelma told me why they had to leave the bayou. It was because of something Clarence did. A couple of years after the war had ended, he threw a fit in the local town council building and was driven out of Vinton the next day.

He and Thelma were accustomed to segregation and living under the domination of the white world, and, according to her, Clarence had never once talked back to a white person. He accepted his lot in life and was one of those people who was tougher than tire casing and who saw racism and the despair that went with it as a personal challenge.

But for Clarence, the war was the great equalizer—or at least it should have been. He'd enlisted in the United States Navy in 1939 as a Mess Attendant, Third Class, which was one of the few rankings open to African Americans back then. By the time he was serving aboard the battleship *West Virginia*, he'd been promoted to Ship's Cook, Third Class.

That was just before the attack on Pearl Harbor.

Enemy aircraft dropped armor-piercing bombs through the deck of the battleship and launched torpedoes into her port side. Clarence's legs were badly burned, and another black sailor, nineteen-year-old Johnny Foster, struggled to carry him through oil and water to the quarterdeck just as another explosion went off.

That was when a large piece of shrapnel—the size of a toaster, according to Clarence—hit Johnny Foster square in the abdomen. He survived, but wished he hadn't. After years of pain and several surgeries to repair the damage, the injuries Johnny suffered did kill him, a week after his thirty-third birthday. Clarence has lived every day since, knowing that by saving his life, Johnny Foster eventually lost his own.

Clarence did everything he could while Johnny was alive. He sent money, and made many trips south to visit him at his mother's place in the Texas Panhandle. Her name was Agnes and Clarence told me that despite being over seventy, she still ran a little curio shop called The Wagon Wheel on Route 66 just east of Amarillo.

"You should see this place," Clarence told me. "It's jammed from the floor to the ceiling with drink coasters, refrigerator magnets, bolo ties, ashtrays, salt and pepper shakers, and flags. And old Agnes, well, she's what you'd call an obstinate maverick—refuses to retire. She'll still be sittin' there when the Interstate finally bypasses her."

Clarence used to go to Amarillo at least once a year while Johnny was still alive, and often he brought Johnny up to Saskatoon to spend time with him and Thelma. Johnny stayed the whole summer once. It was 1951, the same summer Wendy Wood was here. I never met Johnny Foster. I wouldn't remember if I did; I was a baby when he died. But Johnny's photograph had always been staring at me from where it sat on the mantel. Along with his war medals.

"I've got to take those back to his mother," I once heard Clarence tell Thelma when she was dusting and polishing. "He never should have left them to me in the first place."

"He wanted you to have them, because you were there with him at Pearl Harbor. You suffered too." Thelma was right.

"Being awarded a Navy Cross is a huge honor," he said. "It's not the kind of thing you stick in the mail. No, I'm going back to Amarillo with those medals some day."

He never made it. I think it was too painful to go back there without Johnny waiting at the other end with an armful of corny souvenirs. (Damn near every piece of glassware we drank from featured either the Route 66 shield, a picture of a bucking bronco, or a semi-naked lady in a cowboy hat. And the slogan *Don't Mess with Texas* was as common at our place as *Bless this House* was everywhere else.)

Thelma told me it was his experience with Johnny at Pearl Harbor that caused Clarence to throw the fit in Vinton.

"At first," Thelma explained, "Clarence was real happy that the council was mounting a special plaque in the city hall for the boys in service, as they were called in those days."

"What about women?" I asked.

"Oh, plenty of women served during the war, Easy," she said, "but none from Vinton had lost their lives. This plaque was for the young men from the area who had died in the war." She thought for a minute. "Now, where was I?"

"Clarence's fit."

"Well, Clarence and I, and the other servicemen and their families, were having coffee and waiting for the unveiling. When the mayor finally pulled off the sheet, the look on Clarence's face was like nothing I'd ever seen." She shook her head back and forth. "Etched into a background of shining gold

17

plate were the names of the white boys who had lost their lives. At the bottom, on the plain wood, under the heading *Coloreds* was a list of the black men who had died beside them. In small print. Like an afterthought."

"Oh, God," I said. "What did Clarence do?"

"He walked over to that plaque and tore it off the wall. Then he turned to the mayor and said that blacks and whites might have to use different washrooms, and they might have to drink from separate fountains, but the blood that poured out of their wounds aboard that ship at Pearl Harbor was the exact same shade of red."

I never asked Clarence about it. Thelma told me to let it rest, so I did. I asked him once why he moved to Saskatoon— why that would be his choice—and he said that the garage was for sale and that it was the right price. I think it was the farthest place from Vinton he could find.

Once Thelma was gone, the garage was the only thing Clarence had left. And me. That was why I wished he'd move back to the States and take me with him; I knew how guilty I was going to feel when I finally left Saskatoon in the dust. Clarence held on to the ever-dimming hope that one day I would become marvelously efficient at motor mechanics and would decide to apprentice with him; but deep inside he knew that once I had enough money, I'd be gone as sure as yesterday's rainbow. He couldn't blame me; waiting for the blues to come to Saskatoon would be like waiting for the earth to take a radical detour from its regular orbit. He knew I had to go.

By the spring of 1970, Clarence could see that although I

was putting in hours with him and collecting my pay, my heart was not in the garage. I wanted to sing. I needed to sing. And I was going to sing. So he advertised for an apprentice, and by the end of May, along came Larry Alder from Porcupine Plain, a small town about three hours (and thirty years) east of Saskatoon. Clarence said that in his application, Larry wrote about being the seventh son of a wheat farmer on an operation with a mere 1,200 acres, and therefore only enough land for six sons. He claimed to be hardworking, and said that although he knew how to repair tractors and combines, what he really wanted to do was fix cars.

Larry was a year older than me, but it was clear from the beads of sweat on his upper lip that he was nervous when we first met. I figured he'd never been to the city before, and never seen a black girl either, because he stared at the ground when I picked him up at the bus station.

"Didn't Clarence warn you that we were black?" I asked him. "You can change your mind, you know. The bus hasn't left yet. There's still time to—"

"Go home? No, I don't—"

"So he did warn you then."

Larry was confused. "*Warn* me?"

I took a good long look at him. He wasn't bad-looking, and his jeans weren't horrible, but the big brown belt and horseshoe buckle at his waist looked like something he'd found in the back of his grandfather's closet. Larry's shirt was clean. It had obviously gone through hundreds of washes, and it probably had a few weeks of wear left in it before it was ready for the ragbag.

And his hair was cut too short. His mother probably did it on the front porch with a pair of shears.

I tried my question again. "Didn't Clarence tell you that you'd be working for a black man?"

Larry didn't reply, and for a minute, neither one of us said a word. I could tell that he was trying desperately to assemble enough courage to cast the first stone into the pool of silence between us.

"I like black people," he finally muttered.

"Have you ever met one?"

"On television."

"Television?" I asked. "C'mon! How can you meet someone on television?"

He thought about it for a while, then replied, "In Porcupine Plain, that's about the only way you *can* meet anyone."

That made me laugh, anyway.

Larry picked up his suitcases, and we headed to the lot where I'd parked the tow truck. That was when I heard something that sounded like *Meeeee. Meeeeah.*

Then I noticed that one of his suitcases wasn't a suitcase at all. It was an animal carrier, and inside was a small black cat with big yellow eyes, like the gambler Thelma had told me about. I stopped in my tracks.

"Don't you like cats?" asked Larry, following my gaze to the cage.

"Sure. Why not? What's her name?" I stuck my finger through the wire and stroked the middle of the cat's forehead.

"He's a boy," said Larry. "His name's Gilligan."

"Gilligan? From the television show?" I had trouble believing anyone could make it through an episode of that sitcom, let alone name their cat after it.

"Gilligan's Island was my favorite program," said Larry with a smile. "That and *The Munsters*." He opened up the door to the tow truck and placed the cat and his suitcase on the floor next to his feet. "I almost called him Herman, but I like Gilligan better. Gillie for short."

Larry watched out the corner of his eye as I switched gears.

"I've never seen a girl drive a truck before," he said. I thought about reminding him that at eighteen, I was no longer a girl, but figured where he came from, women were probably still considered girls until they'd had their fourth child.

"Clarence told me you're going to be staying at Mrs. Hill's boarding house. Did you tell her you have a cat?"

"Should I have?" Larry's eyes turned dark with fear.

"She's allergic to everything on the planet," I said. "Dust, dander, pollen—me."

I watched Larry's spirits fall with a thud.

"Oh, no," he said.

"And every time she sneezes it sounds like she's shouting *ah-screwyou*." I told him that to cheer him up, but it didn't work. His ears turned scarlet.

"Maybe I'd better head back home."

"Because of Mrs. Hill?"

"Because of Gillie. We've never been apart. Not since the day I found him in the hayloft. She won't want him at her house."

Part of me—the part generated by Wendy Wood—
thought about having a bit of fun teasing the poor wretch
from Porcupine Plain. I could use bad language and watch
him squirm, or tell him stories about wicked city women and
pimps and drugs. But no way could I let him worry about his
cat. What if Thelma was watching me from heaven? She'd be
furious.

"Don't worry, Larry. Gilligan can stay at the garage until
you sort things out. Clarence loves animals."

A look of relief washed over him. But his ears were still red
from me saying *ah-screwyou*.

"Oh," I said, "I'm Easy, by the way."

"You're…easy?"

Now the rest of his face matched his ears.

"My name is Louisiana. Easy for short," I said.

I was enjoying giving him a bad time. Larry didn't talk for
a few miles after that; he muttered little things to the cat and
looked out the window.

By the time we'd pulled into the garage and parked the
truck, I felt guilty for teasing him and tried to be nice. "So you
found Gilligan in the hayloft?" I asked, taking the key out of
the ignition.

Larry nodded.

"Didn't it worry you? You know what they say about a
black cat crossing your path—supposed to be bad luck."

Larry turned in his seat and, for the first time, looked me
square in the eye.

"Should I have *warned* you that Gillie was black?" he said

with a smirk. We both laughed, and that was when I knew that although he'd never be a boyfriend—nothing like that—Larry and I were going to get along just fine.

CHAPTER THREE

The entire month of June was extraordinarily hot, and was made even more unbearable by Mrs. Hill, who—now that one of her boarders was working for Clarence—made her presence felt at the garage daily. She'd drop by with a sandwich and a selection of her homemade pickles for him at noon, then cast an investigative eye over whoever happened to be there, looking for anything she might be able to pass on to her network of spies. She couldn't hang around too long, thanks to Gillie and my music, both of which disgusted her. You could tell by the way she squinted her eyes. The only other time I'd seen her do that was when Thelma had offered her some home-canned tomatoes. She refused them, but not before listing, for our benefit, the symptoms of that silent killer called botulism.

Mrs. Hill always thought of my music as a sign of general degradation; something I would eventually outgrow like acne.

"So will you be going to college in the fall, Louisiana?" she'd ask me. Her puff of gray hair looked like a gone-to-seed dandelion.

"No. I'm going to sing." I reached over to the record player and turned up the volume on Billie Holiday to drown her out.

"My granddaughter has been accepted into teacher's college. She's going to be—"

"A teacher."

"Yes. That wouldn't be of any use to you, of course, but surely you could find some type of suitable program." What she meant was that nobody would hire a black schoolteacher, but maybe I could learn to blow glass or something.

I wanted to blast the music louder, but then Thelma came into my head.

Be gracious, Easy.

Let it go, Easy.

Live your own life and do your best and you'll see how things will turn out right for you.

I kept my eyes focused on the quart of oil that I was pouring into a motor and said nothing. Thankfully, Gillie came over to rub against Mrs. Hill's ankles.

Larry spotted the cat and went to grab him, but I made a face so he'd leave him where he was. Mrs. Hill was about to sneeze, and I waited for the *ah-screwyou,* but she bustled out of the garage instead. "Don't be late for supper," she hollered to Larry.

"How do you tolerate that old crab?" I asked him.

"Mrs. Hill? Oh, she's not so bad once you get used to her." I had the feeling Larry would say the same thing about

25

the bride of Frankenstein. He took the jug of oil from my hand and poured it into the engine for me—help I didn't need, but that was Larry. "She can't cook like my mother, though," he added. And then, looking at his sandwich, he declared, "She mixes cheese whiz into tuna fish."

"Yuck."

"And her pickles are sour."

"No surprise there," I mumbled.

"She keeps the place clean, though," added Larry. "If you dropped a slice of bread and butter on the kitchen floor, then picked it up, you'd never be able to tell which side had landed face down."

I took two sodas out of the cooler and snapped off the lids. "So by now, she must have told you all about me, right, Larry? All the sordid details?"

Larry said nothing. He jammed a pickle in his mouth and reached for the bottle of cola.

"Oh, c'mon," I insisted. "You've been living at her place for a month now. You probably heard about Wendy Wood within the first twenty-four hours!"

"Easy!" hollered Clarence from outside the garage. "Easy, can you come here for a minute?"

"Yeah, yeah, yeah," I yelled back. Then I took a swig of pop. "Well, just for the record, I've never met Wendy Wood and don't want to, okay?"

Larry kept chewing his pickle.

"I hate her. And as for Clarence, I'm sure he regrets—"

"Easy!" shouted my father. "I need you out here! *Now.*"

I folded the waxed paper back around my sandwich and headed out to the parking lot. Boy, did I get an eyeful. There stood Clarence, with a dumbfounded expression on his face, and next to him were two nuns. One of them was dressed in a long dark gray habit and veil, and the other, a younger one about my age, wore a gray jumper, a white blouse, and a small white veil. I figured it was the outfit she had to wear before committing, and I was right.

"This is Sister Beatrice, and this is Marsha Evanko," said Clarence, offering no further explanation as to what they wanted or why they were there. Then he nodded his head and left them with me.

"I'm…uh, Louisiana Merritt," I sputtered, making the snap decision not to use my nickname. Then, for some reason, I asked the younger nun if Evanko was a Ukrainian name, and she nodded her head in the same disinterested way Clarence had just done. I didn't give a damn whether she was Ukrainian or not, but I couldn't think of anything else to say.

I took a rag out of my back pocket and wiped off the grease, in case they wanted to shake hands. They didn't reach out though, so neither did I. Marsha Evanko was thin and greenish, with big, damp eyes. Her limbs were spindly, like she'd been fabricated from pipe cleaners. The older one, Sister Beatrice, looked as if she'd melt at any moment. It was a stifling hot day, and that habit she wore seemed like something overlooked by the Marquis de Sade.

I waited for one of them to speak up, but they just stood there. Finally I resorted to the weather.

"We've had some good days, lately. Nothing but sunshine," I muttered in a *but-I-don't-really-care* sort of way.

"It'll rain soon," declared Marsha Evanko, leaning morbidly on the car beside her. "And a cloudburst will do a lot of damage to the crops." I decided that Marsha was one of those people who was sad and wanted everyone else to be sad, and if you gave her the chance, she would probably point out the many opportunities for failure in any endeavor you might have in mind.

"So…well…what can I do for you?" I asked, glancing quickly at the sky to see if she was right. The only reason I had any patience with them was because they were nuns, and therefore had an in with God. I didn't want to risk getting on their bad side, just in case all my atheistic lemon-gin-drinking pals were wrong.

The nuns looked at their car despondently, at each other knowingly, and at me skeptically.

I asked again.

They didn't say a word.

"Look, I've got work to do. What do you need? An oil change?" I was losing my patience, even if they were religious. I scanned the sky again, this time for any sign of lightning. "I haven't got all day."

"All haste is of the devil," said Marsha, in a voice that could only be described as sepulchral.

Oh, for God's sake. Who the hell does she think she is? I turned to Sister Beatrice, and held my arms out as if to say please tell me what's going on.

"Your father said—the owner of the garage is your father, right?"

I nodded.

"Yes, well, he said that you could spend a few minutes giving us some tips on how to buy a used car. What to look for."

"He did, did he?"

"But…but do you really know about cars?" Again, a suspicious look.

"Yes, I do."

Sister Beatrice smiled and seemed pleased to meet a female mechanic, but Marsha's disapproval stuck out all over her like porcupine quills.

I walked around to the driver's side of their car. "What's wrong with your Impala?" I tried to be upbeat, but wondered who it was that had the nerve to sell two nuns a dark sedan that looked like something a gangster would drive.

I opened the door, reached inside, and pulled the lever to release the hood; Sister Beatrice jumped when it popped open.

"Did it run smooth for a while, then go *chigga-chigga-chigga*, then run smooth again?" I asked. "If so, it's probably a clogged fuel line."

"I can't get it out of first gear," said Sister Beatrice.

"We paid several hundred dollars for this vehicle from a man who came by the convent," added Marsha.

"You didn't have it checked out first?"

Sister Beatrice shrugged her shoulders, as a sort of apology for being so dumb, but Marsha, in a voice that sounded exactly like the receptionist at the funeral parlor, explained that some members of the human race feel that it is okay, preferred even, to lie, cheat, and steal, with no regard for whom it hurts, and that the man who sold them the car was one of those despicable people.

The guy cheated a pair of nuns? He must be either exceptionally brave or hopelessly desperate. Maybe both.

"Mother Superior heard from a member of our church that your father ran an honest garage, so we were hoping you could steer us in the right direction, and help us to find another car," said Sister Beatrice. "We just can't afford to have this happen to us again."

"Again? You mean—"

"This is the third car we've had in a year."

I got in and started up the engine. From the noise I could tell right away that the carburetor was a problem, but that was only part of it. I turned off the motor before the engine got hot, and threw up the hood to take a good look inside.

"Oh, here we go," I said, when I detected sawdust. "Oldest trick in the book."

"What's that?" asked Sister Beatrice.

"Sawdust in the transmission. Makes worn-out gears run smooth for a while, then…well, it's game over. And the cost of repairing the transmission would be more than what the car is worth."

Marsha buried her face in her hands. I didn't feel the least bit sorry for her, but I liked Sister Beatrice, so I decided to help them out.

"Okay, okay," I said. "It's safe to say that every salesman

in this city is going to take advantage of you." I let go of the hood, and it bounced back. It took three times before the thing would lock. "I'll bet the crook who sold you this boat said it belonged to an old lady who drove it only once a week, to Bingo. Am I right?"

The two looked at each other from under their eyelids.

"Right?" I repeated.

"No," replied Sister Beatrice. She bit her bottom lip. "He said it belonged to a sea captain."

"A sea captain?" I laughed at that one. (They didn't.) "All right, if I come with you, I can weed out the hustlers, since they won't suspect that I know anything about cars."

"Oh, wonderful," exclaimed Sister Beatrice. She grabbed Marsha's arm. "We're in luck," she said.

"Why don't you give me a call next week and we'll set something up." I turned to go back to the garage.

"Next week?" The older nun dropped the postulant's arm and stepped toward me. "Oh, dear, we were hoping for tomorrow. Wednesday is a holiday, the first of July, and everything will be closed, so that only leaves tomorrow or Thursday, since we must leave on Friday."

"Oh, Thursday's out," I said. "There's no way I can help you on Thursday. I've been waiting for that day for months." Neither one of them asked me what was so important about that day, so I volunteered the information. "The Festival Express is going through."

They didn't know what I was talking about.

"You know, the *Festival Express!*"

They just stood there, slapping at flies.

"Janis Joplin. The Grateful Dead. The Band. Ian and Sylvia and the Great Speckled Bird, for heaven's sake. They've been holding concerts across the country—they've been traveling by train—and they're passing right through Saskatoon on their way to Calgary."

Marsha's eyes rolled around in her head like marbles in a pinball machine. "Sinners," she proclaimed.

"What?" Now I was getting mad and figured to hell with the fact that she was a nun. "Janis Joplin is the best blues singer in the entire world. Didn't you read the article in *Newsweek*? The writer called her a volatile vial of nitroglycerin. Isn't that terrific? I would kill to be called a—" I stopped myself. "I would do just about anything to be able to sing like her."

"Who's Janet Joplin?" asked Sister Beatrice.

"*Janis* Joplin," said Marsha.

"Who's—Who's Janis Joplin?" I felt like saying "Who's Jesus Christ," but I bit my tongue.

Marsha pulled down the corners of her mouth. "She's a sinful woman who drinks and takes drugs," she explained. In that ultra-square jumper and blouse, her voice forbidding and severe, she was like a cross between Mary Magdalene and the county sheriff. "She's only twenty-five, but she's so haggard you'd think she was twice that age."

"Have you ever heard any of her records?" I asked. "And she's twenty-seven, by the way."

"We don't listen to music," said Marsha. "Except for hymns."

Just hymns?

Although I wanted to make Marsha pay for her attitude, the fact that she had nothing but hymns in her life made me pity her, so I didn't carry through on my initial instinct to take off and leave her with the useless sedan.

"So where are you going on Friday?" I asked, my voice brimming with disgust because they didn't like Janis Joplin.

"Albuquerque," said Marsha.

"The Sisters of Charity operate an outreach mission in New Mexico," explained Sister Beatrice. "It's one of the most successful in America, and our Mother Superior would like Marsha to observe their work, with me as her guardian. Then, in October, after she takes her first vows, Marsha will be assigned to work in an inner-city mission in Calgary." She paused. "By the time she takes her final vows, she will know where God wants her to go."

"Oh," I said.

I already know where I'd like her to go.

"After my final vows, I will be sent to wherever I am needed the most."

"Oh," I repeated.

"Yes, wherever I am needed the most."

"So," I said, wishing I hadn't offered to help them in the first place, "it looks as if tomorrow's the only day we have to find you a car. Let's hope there's something out there."

"I have faith," said Marsha, sounding like she was about to be wheeled into an operating room.

"We'll be here promptly at noon, if that's all right," said

Sister Beatrice, as the two of them got back into the sedan. "And God bless you," she added. They drove off in first gear, but still managed to produce a cloud of dust.

I went back inside the garage and was going to give Clarence a piece of my mind, but he spoke first.

"I know you've been thinking about buying a car—to get you to New Orleans," he mumbled, never taking his eyes off the fan belt that hung around his left wrist. "This way you can check out the dealers."

"Yeah," I said. "I do want to see what's available. I'd like to find a nice classic convertible that I could fix up. Something like Billie Holiday would drive."

"Yeah."

He sounded dejected. I knew it was because I'd soon be leaving town, so I shut my mouth and went back to work without mentioning the nuns. Gillie was watching Larry clean the gunk out of a starter motor, Bessie Smith was singing "After You've Gone," and I wondered how I managed to get so involved with Sister Beatrice and that horrible Marsha.

Thelma always said that everything happened for a reason. I hoped like hell she was right.

CHAPTER FOUR

It wasn't just the powdered sugar on his chin that steered my decision—I had no intention of going out with Larry anyway. I knew it was only a matter of time before he invited me somewhere, so when he finally got up the nerve, I had already rehearsed my answer. It was a lengthy explanation culminating in the fact that since we were working together, it wasn't a good idea to become involved romantically. I had examples, too. There was the woman around the corner who ran a butcher shop with her husband. After years of keeping their fighting down to quiet slaps, hissed slurs, and the occasional threat with a meat cleaver, she finally couldn't stand him any longer. The sight of her wedding ring was making her sick. It wouldn't budge, so she tried sawing it off and almost lost her finger in the process.

And there was the couple who ran the Laundromat, three doors down from our garage. They started out great, and business was good. After a while, though, they fought every time there were enough machines running to drown out the noise. And then, just before Christmas, the woman ran off with one of the customers because he told her she was a flaming hibiscus. (According to the Laundromat division of Mrs. Hill's spy agency, he was from Quebec and wore nothing but red underwear.)

If I'd had a boyfriend, I would have been provided with an automatic excuse, and the exposition would have been unnecessary. No white guys, however, had the guts to go out with a black girl, even one who was half white, and thanks to Mrs. Hill, everyone within a ten-mile radius was well acquainted with my sordid origins as the daughter of a drifter. I didn't care. I figured that once I got out of Saskatoon, there'd be plenty of men who didn't fear social alienation by asking me out.

Despite my best efforts at letting him down easy, I crushed Larry's ego like an eggshell.

"Here," I said, passing him the box of doughnuts, "have another. Please."

He didn't.

He just picked up Gillie and stroked his back.

"You do understand what I'm saying, don't you?" I asked.

"I thought maybe you'd like to go to a wedding, that's all." His voice was dripping with disappointment. "My brother Lyle and his wife, Skeeter, are coming all the way from Porcupine Plain and—well, I wanted them to meet you."

"Skeeter?"

"She's a little mite of a thing. Flits around all day like a skeeter, that's how she got the name."

"Oh, like a mosquito," I determined.

"She was born right here, in Saskatoon—like you," added Larry. "Her parents moved to Porcupine Plain when she was little, but she still thinks of the city as her home." I guess he hoped that fact would help his cause. It didn't, so he put down the cat, then turned on the portable black-and-white television set we kept in the garage. *The Beverly Hillbillies* was on, and while he would normally laugh hysterically at what I thought was the stupidest show in the world (next to *Gilligan's Island*), this time he continued to wipe down his wrenches with oil and never cracked a smile. He looked so solemn, I felt like handing him a pistol and leaving the room so he could take the only way out. I went back to my work instead, but the unbearable silence and intolerable television show drove me to ask the burning question:

"So, if you are Larry and your brother is Lyle, do the other five boys all have names beginning with an *L*?"

He kept his gaze on the wrenches, but answered my question.

"Leonard, Lester, Lloyd, Lance, and Louis."

"Oh."

"I told them all about you. Changing gears and everything."

"Changing gears? They must be fascinated." *Why didn't you tell them that I sing?*

Clarence came in the side door of the garage carrying a box of supplies.

"So…uh…did you tell them that I sing?" I asked Larry.

"What time do you leave?" interjected Clarence, his eyes grazing the clock on the wall.

Larry looked at me, and I could tell he wanted to ask where I was heading off to, but his self-respect had taken too much of a beating. I told him anyway.

"I got trapped into helping a pair of nuns from the convent near St. Paul's hospital. They've been gypped a few times by shifty salesmen." I rolled my eyes and sighed mightily. "I have to help them find a car. And it had better be today, because nothing's open tomorrow, and I'm taking Thursday off because Thursday is the most important day in my whole life and nobody, or nothing—did you hear me, Clarence?—nobody or nothing is going to interfere!"

I waited for Larry to ask me what was happening on Thursday, but he started taking the headlight out of a pickup truck with a loud electric drill. "She's gonna need new cables," he hollered to Clarence.

He's ignoring me because of that damned wedding. Why would he think that I would be interested in meeting Lyle and Skittles—or whatever her name is? Just the thought of them bores me to death.

"Larry?" I said. "Look, I'm sorry but—"

He put down the drill, waited for Clarence to go back outside, then took an almost-trembling breath. "It was dumb of me to think that you'd…well, that you'd go out with me."

That did it.

That made me feel so guilty about turning him down that

I couldn't stand to look at my own reflection in the side mirror of the truck.

"Here," I said, handing Larry a tissue. "There's sugar on your chin."

He wiped it off, threw the tissue in the trash, and began fitting a new bit into the end of his drill.

I helped myself to a cruller. "Well, uh…it's been a long time since I've been to a wedding, actually." I fumbled to find the words. "Thursday's out, that's for sure…but I guess the wedding's on—"

"Saturday night." He beamed. "You mean you'll go?"

"Yeah, Larry, I'll go." I swallowed a big piece of doughnut and an even larger chunk of pride. "Can't wait to meet Skooter."

"Skeeter. She's a hoot. You'll love her."

♫

On the stroke of noon, Sister Beatrice and Marsha arrived in the big sedan. Clarence offered us the tow truck, but I couldn't imagine the three of us squeezing into the cab, especially with that bulky habit of Sister Beatrice's taking up so much space.

"First gear is good enough to get around town," I said. And then, digging deep to find the last dribble of good cheer I had left, I mumbled, "All aboard." Thanks to a dull wedding ahead, and the prospect of a whole afternoon with two nuns, my voice held the same wild enthusiasm generally bestowed on process servers and bill collectors.

Marsha's nose was running and her veil was tightly secured with bobby pins, crossed like swords. Sister Beatrice thanked me again for my trouble. Neither of them was in any way prepared to face shifty-eyed, self-confident con artists, as evidenced by the fact that on our very first stop, they were shown the exact same car they were driving and didn't even realize it.

"She's a dilly," said the salesman, taking us to a dried-blood-colored sedan. "Runs like a clock." He wore a wrinkled suit, had a large dandruffy part in the middle of his head, and black tufts of hair in his ears. The three of us followed him to the car—the nuns out of naiveté, me out of curiosity.

"I can give you this baby for four hundred clams," he said, kicking the back tire as if he was trying to wake the thing up. Sister Beatrice and Marsha turned to me, and I shook my head.

"Thing's not worth fifty bucks," I said, opening the driver's door. On the seat was a spilled bottle of nail polish, congealed into a shiny gob, and a paperback copy of *Debbie Surrenders*. Marsha turned away in horror, Sister Beatrice looked at the ground, and the car salesman yelled "Whoops," pushed me out of the way, and slammed the door shut.

"Let me show you a terrific 1961 Nash Metropolitan. It's a winner, a real beauty." He pointed to a two-tone wreck dozing on the edge of the lot. "Caribbean Blue with a Misty Beige contrast. Beautiful."

"A Nash Metropolitan!" I exclaimed. "Like we'd ever be able to get parts for one of those dinosaurs. They haven't rolled off the assembly line in years!"

"We have parts, we have parts—"

"Like hell you do," I said. I looked over at Marsha, who was scowling at me for swearing. "Sorry," I said, but I wasn't.

"Okay, what about a '55 Packard Clipper," he tried, heading to the other side of the dealership.

We followed behind him like ants, but I knew before we got there that a fifteen-year-old car would never do. After that, the four of us crisscrossed the lot ten times, and saw a specimen of every automobile ever produced, but not one was fit to drive the nuns to the grocery store, let alone Albuquerque.

The next place we hit was every bit as bad. A large, gray man with little pools of spit in the corners of his mouth took us inside to tell us about the various and sundry terrific buys he had, and even offered a twenty-percent discount, since it was for the church. I had a hunch that he'd already added on twenty-five, thinking that everything the three of us knew about cars, when tallied up, could be written on the head of a pin.

His office was as stuffy as Miss Poultice's parlor, with oil cans and magazines and bills of sale scattered haphazardly from one concrete wall to the other. He pushed three stools close to his desk, then threw himself into a swivel chair and leaned way back.

All of a sudden, his eye caught something on the wall behind us, and he jumped up out of his seat. It was a Playboy calendar, and he tore it down so quickly that part of Miss June's left breast was still hanging on the nail, dangling back and forth like a sign in a sex shop window. He wasn't fast enough, though; we all got a good look at the red-headed beauty. Every part of her.

Sister Beatrice wrinkled her forehead in a puzzled kind of way. Marsha stood up, crashed her stool against the desk, and marched outside. The salesman scratched nervously like a little mouse.

"Okay," I said impatiently. "Have you got any late-model cars? Something in excellent shape that'll get these ladies to New Mexico without a hitch?"

He took Sister Beatrice and me back outside to see a 1961 Ford Falcon. We walked past the nuns' car, and its windows had all been rolled down. Inside was Marsha, staring straight ahead, ignoring us like a bored and sulky pre-teen.

I protested that the car was nine years old, but the man—figuring I didn't know the first thing about automobile mechanics—gave me the business.

"Yeah, but low mileage," he said, as he tried to force open the passenger door. "This doll hasn't left Saskatoon." He gave the door another pull. "She's been sitting in the owner's garage for six of those nine years. At four hundred and fifty bucks, we're just giving it away. Just giving it away."

I threw open the hood and told him the doll was going to need plugs, a radiator hose, a water pump, ignition wires, and a starter switch, and more than likely brake shoes, brake drums, and brake linings—I couldn't tell without getting underneath her. He reduced his eyes to squinting pinpricks and accused me of being sent by another dealership to spy on him and his cars.

"What?" he hollered. "You think I'm stupid? I knew all along that you were some kind of weird girl-expert in cars. And those nuns are foils. Sure they are. Well, you can go right back to whoever sent you here and you can tell them to—"

"Look, Mister," I said. "I'm just trying to find a decent car for a reasonable price. Period. I have nothing up my sleeve."

He thought for a minute or two, then his expression changed, and he became hysterical with mirth. He laughed and laughed and laughed. I looked at Sister Beatrice and she shrugged. Then the salesman began to search frantically for a television camera.

"I get it. I get it now! Ha, ha, ha. Nuns. A girl mechanic!" He laughed again. "I'm on that television show!" His eyes searched the lot wildly. "Where's Allen Funt? C'mon, where is he?" He took off running from car to car, and was still trying to find the host of *Candid Camera* when we pulled off the lot.

CHAPTER FIVE

If it hadn't been the color of a ripe banana—golden-yellow with the occasional spot of brown—the six-year-old Pontiac station wagon would have been the perfect choice. It had only one previous owner (verified), and when I inspected the engine, everything was sound. Anyway, we were out of options; the dealership where we found it was the last one on our list. And the color, it turned out, gave me some bargaining power.

"Six hundred dollars?" I gasped. "Oh, give me a break. This thing's so bright it could tan your skin."

He looked at my arm, then raised his eyebrows, forcing me to explain.

"I said *your* skin." (Which was white all right, but not even close to Marsha's just-got-out-of-jail-after-thirty-years white.)

The salesman was a nice sort of guy, although he had a tendency to punctuate every sentence with a nudge or a wink.

I didn't want to cheat him, but the car was for the church, and therefore for God, so I figured I'd better get the best price I could.

"C'mon, little lady," he said, elbowing my side, "you're a smart cookie. You know this is a good buy."

"Um, I'm not sure," I said. "What do you think, Sister Beatrice? Should we try out a few other places first?"

She got into the driver's seat and bounced up and down, like she was trying out a bed or a sofa in the furniture section of a department store. Then she put her hands on the wheel and pretended to be driving, much like a kid would on his father's knee.

"Oh, it's wonderful," she beamed, until I made a face to warn her not to appear over-eager. "Well," she hedged, "I mean it's…well, it's…" She thought for a second. "Do you have one in Caribbean blue?"

"Nice try, nice try," said the salesman with a wink. "No, I'm afraid we're all out of Caribbean blue today." Then he elbowed me again. "How about a test drive, eh? Take her around the block." He laughed. "It's not like I have to worry about you stealing it. Ha, ha."

Sister Beatrice shoved over so I could take the wheel. Marsha sat in the backseat, rested her elbow on the door handle, and stared out the window. "What a perfectly hideous color," she said fractiously.

"It's a lovely sunshine yellow," said Sister Beatrice, which only made Marsha more dour than she already was.

"As long as it allows us to do the Lord's work, we will have to accept—"

"Look, we've been to every used-car dealer in Saskatoon. You can get it painted later." I rolled down the glass beside me. "Try to think of it as a yellow submarine." I looked at Marsha in the rearview mirror; her nose was still running, and her eyebrows were stitched together. I didn't know what was bugging her, and figured that since it was doubtful I could change her disposition, the only thing left to do was bug her some more. I started to sing:

> *In the town where I was born,*
> *Lived a ma—*

"What a beautiful voice you have, Louisiana," said Sister Beatrice. "Doesn't she have a wonderful voice, Marsha?"

"I hate the Beatles," was her reply.

"Nobody hates the Beatles." I pulled the car out of the lot and onto the main drag. The main drag, however, turned out to be Marsha, and after a few miles of her vacillating between hating everything on the one hand, and accepting everything as the will of God on the other, I decided to turn around. The nuns bought the car—I managed to get the salesman to knock a hundred bucks off—and Sister Beatrice drove it back to the convent. But not before thanking me profusely for my help.

"No sweat," I said. "I was looking around for myself, too. Didn't find my dream convertible, though."

"If there's ever anything we can do for you—"

"Just put in a good word for me. You know, with the Big Guy." Sister Beatrice smiled as she drove off in the station wagon, leaving me with Marsha and the old sedan in first gear. At least when she dropped me back at the garage, I could wave a hearty good-bye, knowing that I'd never have to spend another afternoon with Marsha, the petulant postulant, again.

That's what I thought, anyway.

♪

Wednesday, the first day of July. Dominion Day. The garage was officially closed, although Clarence kept himself occupied by doing some bodywork on a '37 Buick that one of our regular customers was restoring to its original condition. Gorgeous car, but Clarence never used to like bodywork. Too fiddly. Too slow. That was before he lost Thelma. When she was in his life—when he had a life—Clarence loved his days off. Loved to take her for a picnic lunch, or go for a long walk in the park, or make ice-cream sodas and listen to music all day. Now he hated holidays. Didn't even acknowledge them. Just worked through them like he would any other day.

Clubs were allowed to stay open, so I decided to try my luck once again. I took the bus over to Saskatoon Blues and stood outside the front window for a while, taking deep breaths and rehearsing in my mind how I'd ask the manager if I could sing for him. After a few minutes, I pulled on the heavy oak door, but it was locked. I should have known a place like that wouldn't open until the evening. So I peered in through the leaded glass to see if I could get someone's attention; that's when I noticed three people inside, not far from a huge mirrored bar.

A woman stood with a clipboard, writing down whatever it was that two men in suits were talking about. She was an attractive blonde in a sundress and high heels, and the men looked wealthy. I guessed they must own the place; one of them, anyway. Maybe the other one was the manager. I thought it best to wait until they had finished their discussion; it seemed important, and I didn't want to make a pest of myself.

I stood sideways behind one of the pillars by the door; they couldn't see me, but I was able to watch them. While I waited for them to wrap up their discussion, I scanned the club. It was beautiful. I'd looked in the window before, but never really taken the time to check it out thoroughly. Every surface was reflective—either glass, or metal, or highly polished wood—and light bounced in all directions. I couldn't see all of the stage from where I was, but I noticed that it was slightly elevated and featured a magnificent grand piano. The bar where the three of them were talking ran the entire length of the building, and was so much nicer than the one at The Beehive. Thelma had promised that she'd bring me here, once I was eighteen; I knew that walking through those doors without her was going to kill me.

You've got to, Easy.

I surveyed the opposite side of the room, where the tables were being set with linen cloths by a guy in a fancy waiter's outfit. The blonde woman said something to him and he nodded, then the two men in suits left. I lifted my hand to knock, but when the waiter moved to the next table, I was starstruck by the photographs on the wall behind him—a lineup of all the singers who had appeared at the club. Many of them were black; all of them were fantastic.

That was when I spotted a picture of Billie Holiday. In the photograph, she was standing next to the man who had just left the room. He was younger-looking then, but it was definitely him.

Billie Holiday played here. Must have been fifteen years ago.

I stared at the photograph for a long time. A long time. Then it hit me.

If they've had people like her sing here, I don't have a hope in hell. Not a hope in hell.

The blonde headed toward the front door, and when she opened it, I decided to give it my best shot.

"Hi," I said. "My name is Louisiana Merritt and I was wondering if I could audition some time. When you have a few minutes." I stopped. "I'm a singer."

She smiled, but it was one of those *Gosh. I'm so sorry, but...* kind of smiles. "We aren't really looking for anyone at the moment," she said, then she looked at her clipboard and set off down the street. I hesitated for a moment, thinking I might try talking to one of the men in suits, but the woman turned and glanced at me.

Anyway, I didn't have a hope in hell.

I got back on the bus and made my way to The Beehive. I hoped that the owner, George Penn, would be in a helpful mood, but wouldn't have bet on it. He wasn't an accommodating sort of guy. Still, I knew that if he'd ever let me sing once, his customers would want me back. Didn't even have to be a weekend. Monday would be fine. Tuesday would be fine. Anything to get me started. Anything so I could leave busking at the liquor store to somebody else.

A blast of stale smoky air hit me when I pushed open the door. The floor was sticky from beer, and a woman with an industrial-sized mop and pail was making her way around the tables, slowly and resentfully swishing underneath them with murky water, then dumping the ashtrays into an old ketchup can. Her droopy, sad-looking cardigan hung to her knees, apparently pulled down by the weight of its own misery.

"What is it?" she said, thrusting her mop into the water with a splash.

"I was wondering—I would like to speak to the owner, is he here?"

She gave me a stony stare.

"Can I speak to him?" I asked.

"Forget it," she said. "You'll have to chloroform me first. You're not gettin' my job." She figured that since I was black, I was a shoo-in for floor cleaning and toilet scrubbing.

When I didn't reply, she came at me with the mop.

"I'm not here for a job!" I exclaimed, and she lowered her arm.

"What are ya here for then?"

"Well, I do want a job—"

She came at me again.

"Hold it, lady!" I moved to the other side of a dirty table. "A singing job. Singing."

"Oh," she said. Then she pointed at the door to the back

room. It had a small circle of glass in the middle; a peephole
of sorts, although it was coated with a thick layer of grime, so
I doubted anyone could see through it.

I knocked softly on the door.

"I'm busy," came a voice from inside. I recognized it as
belonging to George Penn. "Get lost," he said.

"It's Louisiana Merritt. Can I see you for a minute?"

"I'm busy." Then he added, "If this is about Clarence's bill,
I told him I'll pay it next week. It's too high anyway."

"Mr. Penn, I'd like to have a chance to audition for you.
If you'll take a minute to hear me sing, I think you'll realize
that I—"

"I told you before, you're not good enough."

"You've never heard me sing!" I hollered through the crack
in the door. "How do you know I'm not good enough?"

"I just do."

"Look, if this is because of Wendy Wood and what happened with Clarence—C'mon, that was nearly twenty years
ago. Nobody cares now."

He said nothing.

"You're afraid that your customers will drink their beer
somewhere else? I doubt it." I thought for a minute. "It's 1970,
for God's sake. People are open-minded now, right?" I pushed
harder. "If you don't want me to audition here, how about coming by the liquor store sometime. I sing on Friday and Saturday
nights. It's just around the block. You can probably hear me
from here if you stand outside—"

"Beat it, kid." He turned up his radio.

I figured if I stood there long enough, he'd click it off eventually, thinking that I'd left. So I sat down on the wet floor (still sticky, despite having been swiped with the mop) and leaned my back against the door.

After a few minutes, George turned the radio off, as I guessed he would. I was about to start begging again when I heard a second voice from inside the office. It was a female voice; probably one of the waitresses.

"…and she thinks she's gonna sing here. I don't want no goddamn bastard half-breed grease monkey…"

Half-breed grease monkey?

I didn't think George Penn was a racist. I figured he was just like everyone else in town and didn't want to stir up the whole Wendy Wood thing again. But I was wrong. He was a plain old bigot. And that was why he wouldn't let me sing.

Never give up, Easy, said Thelma in my mind. *No matter what they call you, no matter how hard it gets, never give up.*

"I'll be back," I told George Penn, even though I knew he couldn't hear me.

I walked past the bar on my way out. There must have been fifty or sixty different bottles of booze lined up behind the bartender, who was getting things ready for the night. He was a young guy, not much older than myself; he had the radio tuned in to a rock station while he cut up lemons and limes. He dried glasses with a cloth, then hung them upside down in a rack over his head. He nodded at me, and I nodded back.

One day, I told myself, *he's going to be serving drinks to a full house while listening to this half-breed grease monkey sing the blues.*

CHAPTER SIX

By Thursday morning, I felt like a skyrocket about to explode. Waiting for the Festival Express had meant a week of confused dreams involving trains that never arrived, standing at the wrong track in the wrong city, and not being able to find my shoes; so when the day finally came, my hands were all fluttery and unmanageable. And trying to keep my mind on engine repairs was impossible, especially with Larry constantly humming the theme song to *Gilligan's Island* under his breath.

I figured that I had a fifty-percent chance of spotting Janis Joplin; since she wasn't the kind of person to accept an aisle seat, I knew she'd be at a window. But in order for me to see her, she would have to be riding on the right side of the train. If she was, I'd recognize her instantly. I'd know Janis from the pink and green feathers in her tousled hair.

I had my accordion and frottoir ready to go, perched

on the top of a tool cabinet near the front entrance of the garage. Ordinarily I wouldn't sing outside the liquor store on a Thursday, since people were stingy on weekdays. On weekends they were generous. Once I made fourteen dollars in less than two hours. But since there was no way of knowing exactly when the train was going to swoosh past, I could be waiting all day, so I decided to sing for the afternoon crowd anyway.

Larry glanced at my frottoir.

"My grandma has a washboard just like that," he said.

"It's not a washboard," I replied. "It's a musical instrument."

"Will you play it for me? And sing?" asked Larry, his eyebrows raised in a pleading sort of way, like he was asking for a new puppy. Or like he *was* a puppy, and was begging me for a treat.

"Why don't you come over to the liquor store some night after work? You can throw money at me there."

A strange look came over his face.

"Liquor store?" He sighed while blowing air slowly out of his mouth. "I promised my mother I'd keep a hundred paces from any place with alcohol." He grabbed a tire from the rack and rolled it past me. "She's a worrier."

"She'd never know."

Larry thought for a minute. "Yeah," he said, "but I would."

"Won't there be liquor at this wedding we're going to on Saturday?" I wondered.

"Oh, gosh no," said Larry. "They're all Baptists."

Oh, my God. A wedding with no liquor, a bunch of Baptists—and Skooter. How did I get myself into this?

Larry looked weird again, then stepped backwards to the

red metal chest of drawers where he kept his screwdrivers and drill bits. When he thought I wasn't watching, he checked behind it like he was worried about spies or termites or something. Then he walked back to where I was working and in a big loud nervous voice, said, "Why don't you play the washboard and sing for me now?"

It was nearing eleven.

I wanted to be trackside by noon.

I put down the starter motor I was repairing. "Maybe another time," I said. "Right now, I've got to get cleaned up." I headed to the stairs that led up to our apartment. Larry grabbed my sleeve.

"Oh, c'mon," he urged. "I want to hear you. It'll be practice for when you meet with those famous people today."

"I'm not meeting them, Larry—just waving to them. If I'm lucky."

"Please." He was clenching his teeth.

"No."

"Please with a cherry on top."

Oh, for heaven's sake! "Okay, but I've only got a minute." I gave in and sang for him, but not with the frottoir. "Here's one from Janis Joplin's *Cheap Thrills* album," I said, and Larry squinted his eyes. I opted for "Summertime."

"Don't worry. It's not dirty," I added, clearing my throat. I started to sing and almost felt myself holding a baby I didn't intend to have, at least for another decade.

Larry liked it—I could tell by the grin on his face—so I kept on singing, and even threw in a little extra vibrato for effect. By the time I'd finished the last verse, though, I sensed that Larry was up to something, and his smile had nothing to do with a passion for Gershwin. He started to giggle like a ten-year-old boy who'd hidden in the bathroom closet to peek at me in the shower. Then he dashed back to his tool cabinet, reached behind it, and lifted up a tape recorder.

"You recorded me," was my matter-of-fact response. I guess I should have pulled his ear and said "You little devil."

"Yup!" He pushed a button, then bobbed his head from side to side while the tape rewound.

Then he played it back. And it sounded good. Really good.

"So where'd you get the recorder, Larry?"

"I borrowed it from Mrs. Hill," he said.

"Part of her surveillance equipment," I surmised. I knew she'd been operating with various spy apparatuses because I'd heard that she'd loaned someone a camera to obtain a photograph of our neighbor's new lampshade. It was pink satin with black lace and had chiffon over top. According to Mrs. Hill, it proved that the woman was up to no good, since her husband's new sales job had taken him to Regina once a week, and a late-model Chevrolet had been seen parked around the corner from her place every time he was gone.

"I don't imagine you told Mrs. Hill what you were borrowing the recorder for," I asked Larry.

"No. She didn't ask, so I didn't worry about it." He smiled. "I wanted to hear how you sound. Everybody always sounds different on tape." He pulled out the plug. "I sound like Elmer Newgast."

"Who is Elmer Newgast?"

"He's the Rawleigh man in Porcupine Plain," answered Larry.

"Rawleigh man?"

"Ointments. Foot powder," he said. "Once, I bought my mom some violet perfume from him."

"Oh," I said. "A salesman."

Larry nodded. "Anyway," he said, "your voice is real pretty. Even on a tape recorder."

"Pretty?" Now there was an adjective I'd never heard applied to music before.

"Yeah."

"I imagine that in Porcupine Plain, everyone listens to country and western, right?"

Larry smiled. "Johnny Cash—now there's a good singer." He stopped. "I mean…like you. As good as you."

I knew Larry meant well, and I was glad that he thought I had a "pretty" voice, but any possible enthusiasm I might have had about his compliment was overshadowed by the realization that in Porcupine Plain, I wouldn't come up to Johnny Cash's bootstraps.

♫

I was surprised that, besides me, two drunks tossing pieces of gravel onto the track, some members of Hare Krishna chanting in a semi-circle, and a small group of Deadheads, there wasn't the huge gathering I'd expected waiting for the Festival Express. All the Hare Krishna guys had close-set, pale green eyes (and

shaved heads) and were high on life; the Deadheads—fans of
the Grateful Dead—wore black T-shirts with skulls and roses
and were high on grass.

One of the drunks beside the track was shirtless; the other
had red wine spilled down the front of a multi-colored blouse
that was obviously made for a woman, since it had darts in the
breast area.

"We didn't miss it, did we?" I asked out loud, hoping
somebody would answer.

One of the drunks leaned toward the other one.

"Did we miss it?"

"Miss what?"

"It."

"I guess."

"What was it?"

"I don't know. I missed it."

Then a Deadhead walked over to me. He emerged from
the cloud of smoke that surrounded his buddies.

"I've been here all morning, so no way we missed it," he
said. "Friend of mine was at the concert in Winnipeg last night
and said the train left there a couple hours after they'd finished."

"You mean in the middle of the night?"

"Yeah, so they'll pass through here around two, I guess."
He took a drag from his joint. The end of it was stained dark
green, and was soaking wet from his lips. I watched as he
inhaled deeply, then *sotto voce* said, "Wanna toke?"

"No thanks." I clunked down my accordion and put the
frottoir around my neck. "So, you're obviously a fan of the

Dead. What about Joplin, do you like her?"

"Great chick," he said. "I'd like to—" He stopped himself. "Great chick."

I nodded in agreement.

Then he hissed, "You're a Janis fan and you don't smoke dope?"

"Can't. Gotta keep my mind clear for singing," I said.

The Deadhead studied my frottoir from every angle, like he was trying to solve a murder mystery. Finally he asked, "What is it?"

"Cajun blues instrument." I played on it for a minute, humming a few bars of a Clifton Chenier song from the bayou. A couple more Deadheads came over.

"Dead started out as a jug band, man," one of them told me.

"No way," I said.

"Yeah. Mother McCree's Uptown Jug Champions. Before they got known by the Haight-Ashbury crowd in San Francisco."

"That's where Joplin started out," I added. "She played with the Dead at Monterey Pop." I glanced over at the semi-circle of chanters. "What are they doing here?" I asked. "They're not Deadheads."

"Yeah, they are."

"What? You're kidding me."

"The Dead had a concert at the Hare Krishna temple in San Francisco—to help them out." He asked the other guy, "Janis played there, too, right?"

"Yeah," he said. "With Big Brother and the Holding Company."

God, I thought. *The things you can learn by the railroad tracks.* "She's with Full Tilt Boogie Band, now," I said. Then I wondered why these Deadheads didn't make their way to see one of the Festival Express concerts. "So why didn't you guys go to Winnipeg or Calgary?"

"No bread, man."

"Yeah," said the other guy. "There was a riot in Toronto over the ticket prices. Jerry Garcia wound up playing for free outside the gates to stop the crowd from destroying the place, man." He watched as I opened up my accordion case and got ready to busk. I threw a few nickels and dimes in there to give people the idea. "Why didn't you go?" he asked me.

"Saving my money for my own career. I'm heading down to New Orleans soon. Gonna sing the blues."

"Far out."

I moved my stuff closer to the doors of the liquor store; although it wasn't busy at that time of day, the odd person sauntered past. I played a full hour of zydeco tunes, interspersed with my favorite Bessie Smith and Billie Holiday songs. Even the Hare Krishna guys stopped chanting at one point and listened to me. And everyone that walked by threw change into my case.

It was when I'd stopped for a break that everything happened. I was sitting with my back against the shady side of the building, looking up at the indifferent blue sky and watching a cloud drift past when I heard the whistle.

The whistle!

I jumped up, grabbed my stuff and ran to the track.

The whistle again!

Oh my God. Here it comes.

Once I heard the thunder of the train's engines, my heart started pounding.

The Deadheads were lighting joints and cheering. The Hare Krishnas were still chanting, but they weren't in unison anymore.

Once it got close enough, I could see the giant yellow letters across the side of the train that read *Festival Express*. My breathing became so shallow I thought I'd drown in my own excitement.

Wow! I scoured the windows for Janis. *Janis? Janis? Where the hell are you Janis? Damn it all, you didn't take an aisle seat, did you? C'mon…look out the window.*

And then the train began to brake.

"They're slowing down!" I screamed to the Deadhead closest to me. "I think they're going to stop!"

He looked at me, and if he hadn't smoked so much grass, his eyes would have been as wide as mine. All his buddies stood in a line, their chins sticking up and out as they scanned the train for the Dead.

And then it happened.

The train stopped. All twelve coaches.

Screech!

At the liquor store. In Saskatoon.

Right where I stood.

And the first person to step off was none other than Janis Joplin.

CHAPTER SEVEN

Janis stumbled when her feet hit the pavement.

"Jeeeesus Key-riste," she hollered, "where the hell am I?" Then she tossed her head and cackled. "I'm in the middle of the goddamn prairies."

Behind her, a huge gang of musicians and managers and sound guys and who-knows-who ambled out of the train, stretched, looked from side to side like they'd just landed on the moon, then headed into the liquor store. They were all at least partially anesthetized, but Janis was further gone than that. She looked like she'd been clipped with an iron bar. It was clear they'd run out of booze, and that was why they'd made the emergency stop, since some guy they called Ken was passing around a shoebox to collect money. Their talk was loud and boisterous and punctuated with claps of laughter—about what, I didn't know—but I had a sneaking suspicion that being stone drunk and finding themselves in Saskatoon might have had something to do with it.

The guy with the shoebox walked right past me, and I heard him call out to Janis about having collected almost four hundred dollars. *Four hundred dollars?* I recognized some members of The Band, and I saw Sylvia Tyson; the only sober one to emerge from the train, she looked lovely in a red mini-dress, her perfectly straight, long dark hair pushed back with a matching headband.

Janis, drunken and braless, wearing gaudy beads and bracelets (and that flock of colored feathers in her matted hair), looked like a cross between a sick old madam and a red-hot hippie mama. If you had tested her blood, it would have been 100 proof. But she stood out so much from everyone around her—and was so far above the rest of us anyway—it was like watching Gulliver with the Lilliputians.

My Deadhead friend skidded over to tell me that he'd gotten Jerry Garcia's autograph on a pack of cigarettes. Before I'd had a chance to take a look at it, he spotted another member of the group—I think it was Ron "Pigpen" McKernan—and ran after him. But when the singer hopped back on the train without so much as a nod, the Deadhead began to droop; that was when I decided not to approach Janis. I didn't want to be shunned. I preferred to register this moment of my life as a rare, exciting one that I could treasure and bring out every once in a while to fondle and remember.

I guess life had other plans, though, because Janis approached me.

Throwing her lips to the left, she yelled to the guy with the shoebox, "Don't forget the Southern Comfort, man." She turned up her bottle and shook it to show him it was empty. Then she pointed at my frottoir and accordion.

"I thought we were in Canada, man, not New Orleans," she said with a twang. She was so Texan you could almost hear her spurs jangle. "Where the hell did you get those instruments?"

No matter how many times I go over it in my mind, I cannot figure out why I replied the way I did. It must have been temporary insanity, but instead of telling her about my musical background in zydeco—and blues, of course—I said, "I saw you on the Dick Cavett Show."

Dick Cavett? Good God. I quickly added, "You were fantastic."

"Thanks, man," she said. Then she came so close to me that I could see right into her glassy eyes and smell her liquor-soaked breath. "So you heard me tell him about my class reunion," she said, brushing back hair and feathers with her hand.

"Yes, I—"

"Can't wait. It's like I told Dick, they laughed me out of class, out of town, and out of the state," declared Janis. "Now I'm going back."

"I can't believe you were unpopular," I mumbled.

"Ha!" she spurted. "Now I'm going back," she repeated. She was about to say something else, but followed my gaze to a tattoo on her wrist. "So you heard me tell Dick about the cat in San Francisco who did this. Great, isn't it?"

I nodded.

"Aren't you going to play that goddamn frottoir for me?" she asked.

I stood frozen. I felt like I was waiting for a sneeze. Janis picked up the instrument and banged on it with her fingernails; everything she did was so cool and everything she touched— including my frottoir—throbbed hopefully. I would have crawled on my hands and knees over broken glass just to be near her. And there she was asking *me* to play for *her!* It was a good thing that my pal, the Deadhead, had given up on Pigpen and made his way over to where I stood. He nudged me and said "G'wan, sing." I felt like a fledgling, teetering on the edge of a nest, terrified, but hoping for a push.

I picked up my accordion, and sang the first Bessie Smith song that entered my head. Oddly, it was "Downhearted Blues," and although I was petrified, I certainly wasn't downhearted. Despite my bad nerves, I must have done a fairly decent job of it because Janis joined in—a vibrant, earthy, unrestrained version of the song that compelled me to stop singing and listen to her instead. She skipped over half the words, missed a few runs, but gave such an effortless performance that mine seemed more like something from one of Miss Poultice's recitals.

"You're good, man," she told me.

I am? Me?

Then she told me *why* I was good. "Chick singers, man, they tend to stay on top of a song, you know? The secret is to get down to the bottom of the melody. You're down there."

"Well, uh—"

"That's why you're good." She pulled a cigarette out of a thin, gold case. "You do a lot of Bessie Smith?" she asked.

"Yes. And Billie Holiday. Thank you."

Thank you? God, that sounded bad.

"I learned to sing by listening to Bessie Smith," she said.

"Me, too," I responded weakly, since next to Janis, how I learned to sing seemed about as important as yesterday's news.

She lit the cigarette and took a long drag. "You know what I'm doing?" She said it in such a way that I knew she wasn't expecting me to guess.

"No. I don't."

Another drag, this one shorter.

"I'm getting a headstone put on her grave."

"Whose grave?" asked the Deadhead.

"Bessie Smith's." By now, there was a gathering of fans around her, including some Hare Krishnas, the Grateful Dead guys, and some I didn't recognize. "Goddamn bastards didn't mark her grave. Goddamn—"

"They didn't?" I asked her.

"Goddamn bastards killed her." She squinted her eyes into a glassy stare and let smoke flow slowly from her nose. "She was in a car accident near Memphis and the ambulance wouldn't take her to the hospital because it was for whites only." She pulled the liquor bottle out of her purse, remembered it was empty, then hurled it over her shoulder. "They took her to a hospital for blacks, but it was too late." She shook her head from side to side. "Ugly bastards."

I didn't have a clue what to say and neither did anybody

else. She turned around to see what had happened to the guys who had gone inside the store. "Where the hell are you?" she hollered into the air.

I remembered Thelma telling me that story about Bessie Smith, how the ambulance had to travel so much farther to get to an African-American hospital. The greatest singer ever, The Empress of the Blues, and they wouldn't even treat her injuries.

"So what's your name?" Janis asked me.

"Louisiana," I said. "But you can call me Easy."

"Okay, Easy. Then you can call me Pearl."

I can? Only her friends call her Pearl. I can call her Pearl!

"Why do you call yourself Pearl?" I asked, then immediately wondered if I should have. "I mean, if you don't mind my asking."

"Ha!" She tossed her head, and the feather boas in her hair flew every which way, framing her face like the snakes of Medusa. "Pearl protects me from the world, honey. The blood-sucking leeches that want to take too goddamn much from me. Great big goddamn chunks of me. Janis has given them all she can. Ya' know what I mean?"

"Well...uh..."

"I cain't give 'em any more!" Her voice was midway between a whine and a wail.

She dragged on her cigarette a couple of times, then her tone changed.

"So, Easy, why do you have Cajun instruments?" she asked. "You from the south?"

"My parents are from Vinton," I replied.

"Jesus Key-riste, you're kidding me!" she roared. "The best live music I ever heard was in Vinton. I crossed the state line every Saturday night to hear those cats—they were terrific." She stared at me for a minute. "Must have been some hell for your parents—everything so goddamn segregated. I never went to those asshole 'whites only' places, let me tell you. The black bars were where the real music was."

I said nothing, but it was the first time in my life that I was actually *proud* to be black. Janis saw it as a plus, and for once, so did I.

The next thing I remember was one of the members of the Full Tilt Boogie Band coming over to tell her that the store was out of Southern Comfort. Behind them, guys I didn't recognize—I guess they were sound men or gofers—were carrying case after case out of the store, and another guy was filming the whole thing. Since the camera crew was traveling with the musicians, I gathered a documentary was being made of the entire tour.

"You mean they've got every sonofabitchin' bottle except Southern Comfort?" She threw her arms in the air. "What kind of a place is this?" The cameraman turned toward her. "And keep that goddamn lens off me. I'm not in the mood."

She started stomping toward the store and I picked up my instruments and followed her. Another guy—maybe one of the promoters—walked past us with a second box, and Janis accosted him.

"Where the hell's the Southern Comfort?"

"None in stock, Janis," he said. One of her band mates

opened up a bottle of red wine and offered her a drink. She tilted it back, took a swig, then spat it onto the ground near my feet. "Goddamn stuff stinks," she screamed. Erratic, headstrong, bitchy even—but Janis had life by the scruff of the neck and made everyone around her seem as dull as botany teachers.

Nobody could calm her down, not even Sylvia Tyson, who tried to console her with the news that they'd cleaned out everything in the store, including a giant display bottle of Canadian Club. Janis told her where she could put the giant display bottle of Canadian Club, and in a shrill, horrified, accusing voice opened the door of the liquor store and let the cashier have it. Sylvia tried again, this time taking her by the arm and suggesting that someone might be able to combine liqueurs and come up with a drink that was similar to Southern Comfort. Janis's reaction was proof positive that what I'd read in *Newsweek* about her being a "volatile vial of nitroglycerin" was no exaggeration. She tore into the singer, calling her idea the worst piece of shit she'd ever heard (since Southern Comfort can *only* be made in New Orleans) and accusing her of being an asshole for suggesting it.

Sylvia Tyson (a Canadian, by the way) took the Texan's shouting like a lady, smiled and walked away calmly—and I discovered the real reason why the north won the American Civil War.

CHAPTER EIGHT

Janis turned to me and crossed her arms in front. "Ain't no way in hell I'm gettin' back on that train without my Southern Comfort." Her voice, husky to that fascinating point just shy of baritone, was so self-assured that I began to wonder where she planned to stay in Saskatoon, and if she'd mind bunking with me in my room over the garage.

Then she cast a speculative eye over me and blurted, "Do you have any at home, honey? I mean, your parents are from Louisiana, right? C'mon—Easy, that's your name, right? C'mon, Easy, would you get me a bottle from home?" She glanced at the train. "There's still time."

"My mother—well, Thelma—she's dead, and my father doesn't drink much," I said apologetically. When Janis started to panic, I felt like a doctor who'd given her the results of a test, and the prognosis wasn't good. "Anyway, my place is twenty minutes from here, so—"

Curses started to fly like sparks from her mouth. They weren't directed only at me, but included the liquor store, the crowd, the prairies, and God. I began to wonder what those Southern Comfort people put in their liquor, and figured it must be a derivative of nicotine and salted peanuts. The Deadhead, having heard the screams, ambled over and offered Janis a joint to bring her down.

It didn't.

Behind her, I saw those huge bees on the roof of The Beehive, and it hit me. I could dash over there and get a bottle! With a triumphant smile I told her my plan, and she hugged me so tight that her feathers went up my nose. Then she realized she had no money.

"I've got no bread on me. Oh, shit, I've got no bread." Her eyes scoured the lot, looking for someone to give her some cash, but everyone was already back on the train. "There's no time."

"I can do it," I hollered over my shoulder, as I felt for money in my pocket. (I always kept a five and a ten-dollar bill with me when busking, in case someone needed change for a twenty.) I ran as fast as I could around the block and to the bar. Being the middle of the afternoon, the place was empty except for one customer, a creepy man sitting alone in the dark. Instinctively, I located all the exits, then made my way past him as he watched me over the top of his beer, his eyes following me like one of those portraits in a haunted house. Nobody, not even the floor washer, was anywhere in sight. I called out for Mr. Penn, but he wasn't around. I grabbed a bottle of Southern Comfort—it was down a few shots, but almost full—then quickly scrawled a note that I had taken it for Janis Joplin. I stuffed a ten-dollar bill with the note under a bottle of Cointreau and took off past the creepy guy.

With a terrific feeling of godly accomplishment, I handed Janis the bottle, just as the train fired up its engine. She guzzled several mouthfuls, then ran to catch it. "I'll pay you back one day," she bellowed.

"Forget it. It was an honor," I said. It was, but it sounded so square the way I said it, I felt like a botany teacher again.

Then she stopped, turned around, and looked at me. "You're really good, you know," she said. "And I'm not saying that 'cause you got me my Comfort." She hopped up onto the train, then dashed over to the window closest to me. She rammed it open and hung out.

"I got no time to find my goddamn purse, but listen—"

"Yeah?"

"Is there any way you can get to Texas by next Friday—the tenth?" She was scribbling something down on a paper, the train was starting to move, and I felt like I was in one of those dreams where your feet are glued to the ground. "Get down to Threadgill's, you hear me?"

The paper flew out the window and I chased it as a gust from the train's engines blew it from my grasp. If it had flown under the wheels, I'm sure I would have risked death or dismemberment to go after it, but happily, it landed in the gravel near my feet.

"Easy?" I could hear Janis's voice, but all I could see was her bangle-covered wrist sticking out, and her hand waving.

"Yeah?" I said, scooping up the slip of paper and jamming it deep into my pocket.

"Don't take any shit from anyone, you hear me?" she screamed.

"Shit?"

"Just tell them Pearl sent you. You'll be okay."

♫

Larry stayed for dinner at our place because Mrs. Hill was holding a meeting of her women's (spy) club and she wanted him out of the house. I tried to make supper, but having just been told by Janis Joplin that I was a good singer, I found it difficult to concentrate on anything as mundane as food. Larry didn't help matters, either. When I tried to tell him and Clarence about meeting Janis and what she'd said, he interrupted me with his mother's recipe for fried potatoes and a speech about why 4-H is such an important club for young people.

"Heads, hearts, hands and health," he told Clarence and me. And then, after a foray into the mission of the group and all the various farm-related activities it provided, he interrupted me again, this time with a list of the ribbons he'd received for his Amber Durum Semolina.

"It's a spring-planted wheat," he explained, "but you still have to leave a little stubble to protect the seeds."

"Janis Joplin told me that I was a good singer, and even offered to introduce me to the guy who started her career, and all you can talk about is *wheat?*" I threw up my arms. "This is Pearl we're talking about. *Pearl.*"

From his position in the middle of the sofa, Gillie dozing on his knees, Larry giggled at the television set and Clarence stood behind him watching. Neither one of them heard a word I said.

"What the hell's wrong with you two, anyway?" I moved in front of the set to block their view.

"Don't swear," said Clarence. "And could you move out of the way, please?"

They were watching a rerun of *The Andy Griffith Show,* and the episode involved Deputy Barney Fife pretending to be a department store mannequin in order to catch a shoplifter. Larry laughed hysterically, then slammed his thighs with the palms of his hands, and my already taut nerves were worn to within a hair's breadth of the snapping point.

"I've got enough money for the airfare one way," I tried to tell my father. "And if I have to *hitchhike* back, I'll—" I figured the word *hitchhike* might provoke him, but it didn't, so I tried a different approach. "Clarence, if you can loan me a couple hundred bucks, I can do this. I have enough to pay for more than half myself, and—"

"Can't do it this month, Easy," said Clarence. "The hoist is broken and I've got a huge order of parts coming in."

"Doesn't anybody care about my career?" I shrieked. "This is Janis Joplin, for God's sake, and she said I was *really good.*"

"I think you're good, too," offered Larry, still laughing at the show. I felt like saying "Who the hell cares what you think?

You're nobody." Then—to make matters worse—he started on about the wedding.

"Skeeter can't wait to meet you. She can't wait to hear you sing."

"Sing? Sing?" I cried. "Who said I'd sing?"

"Skeeter said she's going to—"

And that was when I cracked.

"Skeeter! Skeeter! To hell with Skeeter and to hell with you and to hell with the wedding! I'm leaving. I'm going to get to Austin somehow." Then I brought up Thelma, something I ordinarily wouldn't do because normally I wouldn't want to hurt Clarence. But this time I did. "Thelma—she would have been happy for me," I muttered.

"Thelma would have told you not to get a swelled head," added Clarence.

"You mean you're not going to the wedding?" asked Larry, as I dashed out the door and down the stairs to outside. He got off the couch and hollered to me as I ran down the stairs. "You mean you're not going to the wedding?" I had burst his bubble and taken wicked satisfaction in doing so.

"No. And you two can make your own supper!" I hollered. Then I threw myself onto the lawn and pounded my fist on the ground.

I am going to get to Texas.

I am going to be famous like Janis Joplin.

I hate Saskatoon and I hate Clarence and I hate Larry and I hate his cat.

No you don't, Easy, said Thelma in my mind. I pulled

myself up to a sitting position. *What's getting into you, girl? You've never spoken to your father that way.*

I tried to erase her from my mind, but she reappeared.

Don't get a swelled head, Easy.

That's just what Clarence said she'd say.

I hated truisms. *Pride cometh before a fall* and sayings like that. It's okay for somebody who hasn't got anything to be proud of—people like Marsha, who love to be miserable—but Janis liked me! The most famous female blues singer of our generation liked me! To hell with pride cometh before a fall.

I picked myself up and started walking—to where, I didn't know, but I knew from experience that if my feet were moving, it helped my brain to think. And it worked. By the time I'd made it to Mrs. Hill's place, I had a great idea.

The nuns. They were the answer to my problem. At least they might be, if I played my cards right.

I flew back up the stairs and found Clarence and Larry trying to figure out how to prepare spaghetti, since potatoes involved too much peeling. Larry had an apron tied around his middle, and Clarence was on a stepstool searching for canned sauce.

"Oh, good," said Clarence, "you're back. Then you can—"

"No, I can't," I replied.

Larry cornered me about the wedding again. "Please come with me. Can't you leave for Texas Sunday morning?"

I didn't answer Larry, and turned to my father instead. "Clarence, I need to take the truck for a while."

"When will you be back?"

I didn't answer him, either. I grabbed the keys off the hook beside the door, and was in such a hurry I stepped on Gillie's tail.

"*MEEEEAHHHH*," he screamed. Larry scooped him up, and I scurried down the stairs, hopped into the truck, and made my way to the convent. Thelma tried to enter my mind the whole time I was driving, but I focused on the road and didn't listen to her. I knew what she was going to say, anyway. I knew she was going to tell me to slow down and calm down and cool down.

As it turned out, once I'd reached the convent, everything slowed down, calmed down, and cooled down automatically. To a grinding halt.

I parked as close as I could to the main entrance of the building, which had a dirty gray prison-like facade. An older, sad-looking nun answered the door when I rang. She had a weepy tear-duct in her right eye, and apparently unable to lift her feet, she scuffled with every step.

"I'd like to speak with Sister Beatrice if that's at all possible. Or—well, I guess Marsha Evanko would do. She's a postulant here."

The nun showed me where to sit, then shuffled down the long hall and turned right when she reached the end. The convent was an austere place with oak benches as hard as tombstones and stale air that smelled like a wet cough-drop box. An ancient elevator to the left of where I sat made creaking, wheezing sounds, as if it resented doing its job. What few long, narrow windows there were allowed only single rays of evening sun to penetrate the building.

The corridors radiated from a central point, in the middle of which stood a huge statue of Christ suffering on the cross. I got up and walked over to study it, and found the agony on the face of Jesus disturbing.

Then I noticed someone standing near me in the shadows; she appeared suddenly and silently behind me. She approached the statue, made the sign of the cross, then turned around to face me.

It was Marsha.

"He died for your sins," she explained grimly.

Sins? What sins?

Other than keeping bad company and drinking milk straight from the carton, I hadn't done too many bad things in my eighteen years. If I spent much more time with Marsha, though, I figured I'd soon start dreaming some up.

White and thready-limbed, she reminded me of a kid I sat next to in grade one, who always had a baggie full of jujubes in her desk. She kept it tightly sealed, but every once in a while would pull one out, shove it in her mouth, then quickly close the bag again. Never once did she offer me one. Never once did I ask. Marsha was like that. She gave nothing.

I looked up at Jesus and thought to myself that whereas Marsha clutched her sins to her chest like they were a beloved old shawl and wasn't letting go of them anytime soon, I didn't have time to worry about right and wrong. I was determined to get to Austin and become a big star like Janis Joplin. Even if it meant involving Marsha in my plan. I asked her when she was leaving for New Mexico, and she pulled down her mouth.

In a voice that was as dark and dreary as the convent, she said, "God willing, we will be leaving early tomorrow morning, right after mass. And God willing, we will be at the American border by the afternoon. Why do you ask?"

I was about to say "Because God willing, I'm going with you," but before I could figure out how to break it to her, Sister Beatrice came clipping down the hall. She, too, crossed herself in front of Jesus, then smiled when she saw me.

"Hello, Louisiana," she said. "How good to see you!"

"Good to see you, Sister," I replied.

We all stood there for a minute, then Sister Beatrice broke the silence with a question.

"So what brings you here tonight?"

"Well…uh…remember when you said that if there was ever anything you could do for me, I shouldn't hesitate to ask?"

Marsha looked at me suspiciously.

"Yes, of course," said Sister Beatrice.

"May I come with you to Albuquerque?"

The two of them were stunned. It was as if I'd dashed over, pulled them out of bed, and yelled, "Come on girls, put on your high heels. I've got a few guys waiting for us outside, and we're all going out for martinis."

"Come with us?" asked Sister Beatrice.

"To Albuquerque?" The cup of Marsha's enthusiasm wasn't exactly running over.

"I will pay my share of the gas, and whatever expenses there are. And I can always service the car, should it need—"

"You said it was a good car," snarled Marsha.

"It is…it is."

"Well, now, I don't know…." Sister Beatrice wasn't sure what to say.

"And a third driver will make it easier for you—less tiring," I added as an afterthought.

"That's quite true," agreed Sister Beatrice.

"Why do you want to come to Albuquerque with us?" asked Marsha, sounding more like a one-woman board of investigation than a postulant.

"I have to get to Texas by the tenth because Janis Joplin is going to introduce me to some music people." I said it matter-of-factly, but neither one of the nuns said a word. "Honestly," I added.

"You met her? She talked to you?" Marsha wasn't buying it.

"Yes, yes, yes," I said. "Look, forget it. If you don't want me to come with you, I understand." I headed toward the door, hoping that Sister Beatrice would stop me, and she did.

"We have several places we must visit along the way," she warned, "at different churches and convents. That's why we're driving there. It's not a pleasure trip."

"But you do plan on being in New Mexico by the middle of next week, right? Even with all the stops?"

She nodded. "Wednesday."

"That would be okay. I'd still have time to get to Austin by Friday night."

"I will ask the Mother Superior," she said, "and let you know later this evening. Can I call you at the garage?"

"Thank you," I said. Then I added another incentive: "Remember that it'll be money for the church if I go."

Marsha, to whom misery clung, couldn't stand the thought of anyone having anything to do with a fun-loving, free person like Janis Joplin, and made no bones about it.

"She takes drugs, you know," I heard her tell Sister Beatrice as I was leaving the building. "Heroin."

I took another look at the cross, and hoped that traveling with Marsha wouldn't be quite that bad.

CHAPTER NINE

When I got back to the garage and saw a police car parked in the lot, I thought nothing of it; I assumed it was there to be serviced. I hurried up the back staircase to start packing, since I figured Sister Beatrice wouldn't let me down and would be happy to have another driver on hand. When I opened the door to the kitchen, and saw two cops standing there with stony stares, I knew something was wrong. Really wrong. Larry looked like he was going to cry. He wouldn't, of course, because men in Porcupine Plain listened to Johnny Cash and didn't cry; not even when there was no rain for months and the fields were so dry they cracked. But the expression on his face made me wonder if something had happened to one of his brothers, or—dare I think it—Skeeter.

"No way, no way," he mumbled to the unsmiling, hard-eyed cop. "Easy would never steal anything. You're wrong."

Steal? Me?

"What's going on?" I said, slamming the door behind me. "Clarence?"

"Someone matching your description stole a bottle of Southern Comfort from The Beehive today, Easy." He spoke slowly and clearly. "I told these men—"

"We'll handle this," said one of the cops, while the other got handcuffs ready.

"I did take it! And I paid for it too. Ten bucks, which is more than it's worth. It was an emergency. I left a note. It was for Janis Joplin."

"Janis…Joplin? *The* Janis Joplin?" repeated the cop, in a now-I've-heard-everything tone of voice.

My heart was racing, and my breathing shallow.

"Yes, that's right. She needed it in a hurry. The train was leaving and…" I pulled out the address for Threadgill's that she'd given me, but I guess it didn't prove anything, since they read me my rights.

"You have the right to remain silent when questioned. Anything you say or do may be used against you in a court of law. You have the right to consult an attorney before speaking to the police and to have an attorney present during questioning now, or in the future."

I felt my hands being pulled behind me and the cold metal of the cuffs brushing the back of my arms. "Clarence!" I cried.

"Stop it," hollered Larry. "Don't put those on her." He tried to intervene, but the cop pushed him away.

"If you cannot afford an attorney, one will be appointed

for you before any questioning, if you wish. If you decide to answer any questions now, without an attorney present, you will still have the right to stop answering at any time until you talk to an attorney."

"Let her go," said Clarence. He pulled me away, just before the lock clicked, so the cuffs were still dangling in the cop's hands. "I sent Louisiana over there and I told her to get George Penn to pay my bill, or else. He owes me a lot of money for work done on his car and hasn't made a payment in months. I'll put up with a lot, but I told my daughter that if he wouldn't pay, we'd have to take matters into our own hands. Penn owes me that bottle for the interest alone. More, in fact! Let's go over there and settle this thing right now." He took his jacket off the back of the kitchen chair. "I'll be one minute," he added, throwing open the door that led down to the garage. "I want to bring the bills with me."

"Clarence, you can't—"

"Be quiet, Easy. Leave this to me."

"The girl will have to come with us," said one of the cops.

"Why?" asked Clarence. "It's my fault. Arrest me."

Why is Clarence taking the blame? He doesn't have to.

"The girl is still under arrest," said the other cop. "We won't use cuffs, but she'll have to stay with us."

Larry put his arm around me, like it was the wing of a mother bird. "I'm coming too," he said. "I'll ride with you in the police car."

"That won't be necessary," said the cop.

"I'm coming. You can't stop me. I'll go with Clarence then."

I ducked down in the back of the cruiser, for fear Mrs. Hill would see. If she spotted *me*—the product of Wendy Wood—in police custody, she'd assume that I hadn't really been saving money by busking, but in fact, was operating as a fairly successful prostitute. I felt my face crumpling, and was ready to cry, but held back for fear that tears would make me look guilty. I wanted to tell the truth, but Clarence told me to do as he said, and anyway, maybe it was a crime to take something without telling the owner, even if I did pay for it. And Clarence did have a case against George Penn—he owed us for our work. We had the right to demand interest. It was printed right on the invoice.

Larry and Clarence arrived at The Beehive before I did, and were already inside by the time the cops escorted me in. It was strange to see the two of them in a nightclub; Clarence detested public places, and Larry promised his mom he wouldn't go near bars. I asked the cops if I could please walk in front of them, rather than have them on each side. They did as I asked, but walked so close behind me, everyone in the place must have known that I was under arrest. The Beehive wasn't brimming with customers, but there were plenty of eyes on me, and plenty of mouths whispering about the black girl, wondering what crime I had committed, and making bets as to how I had run afoul of the law.

"As far as I'm concerned George," said Clarence, still determined to take the rap, "you owe me a lot more than one bottle of Southern Comfort."

"It's against the law to have your daughter enter my business and steal from my bar," he said calmly, like he knew that my father—a black man—didn't have a hope in hell of getting the police on his side. "What if *you* owed *me* money? Would I go over to the garage and help myself to some cash?" He snickered and turned his back on Clarence.

"I pay my debts," said my father, "on time." He slapped the invoices down on the bar.

"Get lost," muttered Penn. "Get back to your carburetors, Clarence."

My father stood strong, like Sidney Poitier in the movie *In the Heat of the Night*. Thelma and I had gone to see it a couple of years before; she cried when Poitier's character, Virgil Tibbs—a detective from Philadelphia—stood up for himself against horrible discrimination in Mississippi. When we watched the movie, I knew that Thelma was comparing his strength to that of Clarence, because I was too. They put Virgil down, called him *boy*, then mockingly asked him what people called him up in Philadelphia. His reply, "They call me *MISTER* Tibbs," has stuck in my mind ever since. Standing there, watching Clarence face George Penn's nasty remarks, I imagined my father walking over to him, turning him around, and saying "You can call me *MISTER* Merritt."

He didn't. He wouldn't.

Instead, he continued making his case to Penn, even though the man's back was still turned, and told him that he had two choices: either drop the charges against his daughter, or expect to see him in small claims court, where Clarence would collect everything owed to him, plus interest, and lawyer's fees on top of that.

At that point, the cops intervened, and asked Penn what he wanted to do.

I felt so bad for Clarence. He kept his gaze on the floor, never making eye contact with anyone in the bar. He rubbed his knuckles nervously. Everyone gawked. It was Vinton all over again, and I couldn't stand it one more second. Thelma would have been horrified.

While the cops were preoccupied with Penn and the invoices, I made my way to the far end of the bar.

"I'll have a…wh-whiskey sour," said a drunk, his words slurring together worse than Janis's. "No ice."

I ignored him and ducked along the bar until I came to where I'd left the money. Sure enough, right where I'd put it, I could see my note and the ten-dollar bill sticking out.

"There it is, Mr. Penn," I hollered. "There's the money, and there's the note." I pointed to the Cointreau bottle not far from where he stood.

The cops came behind the bar, picked up the cash and read the note.

Penn mumbled something about being too busy to notice it.

Then he got mad.

"What's all this crap about my bills then? You never told your daughter to take that bottle. You're full of it!"

"I'm sorry, Clarence," I said, "I just couldn't let them treat you like this." I grabbed his arm. "I'm sorry."

Larry said, "See. I told you she was a good girl."

Oh, stop calling me a girl, for heaven's sake.

The cops asked Penn what he wanted to do, since technically, I had taken the bottle without asking him. He had no choice but to drop everything. No way did he have the funds to pay Clarence, and by that time, he just wanted us out of his bar.

"But I don't want to see your—"

I think he was going to say *black ass,* but held back because the officers were there. He changed it to: "You're not welcome in my establishment anymore." He pointed at me. "And don't you dare ask me again about singing here, or I'll—"

"If you set foot on these premises," one of the cops told me, "you will be charged with trespassing. Do you understand?"

I nodded.

The people at the nearest table twisted their necks to get a good look at me; I was humiliated. Clarence was humiliated.

The other officer warned my father not to meddle with police investigations; he could have been charged with interference, but because he'd never been in trouble with the law before, they agreed to let him off the hook, thank God.

Then the cop cautioned me about stealing things and leaving notes, told me I was no longer under arrest, and escorted me out. Larry and Clarence followed behind, and I hoped and prayed that nobody in Mrs. Hill's espionage group had seen what had just transpired. I doubted that her friends would be in the club, and I trusted Larry not to say a word, but still worried nonetheless. My father wanted to get out fast, too. He kept his head down and walked quickly. Larry, on the other hand, looked from side to side, taking in the sights and sounds of the club like he was on a bus tour of Las Vegas.

"Smoky, isn't it?" he said with a little choke once we were outside. Then he added, "Let's go for a soda. My treat."

A soda? After this?

There was no room left in my stomach after swallowing so much pride.

Clarence declined Larry's invitation, and so did I. The three of us crammed into the cab of the tow truck and drove solemnly back to the garage. Nobody said a word, but Larry whistled all the way back. He started with what I thought was a medley of Johnny Cash tunes, and ended up with "When the Saints Go Marching In."

The mention of saints got me thinking about Marsha and Sister Beatrice, and I felt guilty for having to leave with them the next morning after everything Clarence had done to protect me. I was glad he had Larry. At least with him and Gillie in the garage, he wouldn't be lonely during the day. Still, it would be the first time since Thelma passed that I wouldn't be there to make Clarence his breakfast.

This is the chance of a lifetime.

Surely Clarence wouldn't expect me to give up a career in music just so that I could stay in Saskatoon and make his meals.

I went over those two thoughts in my mind dozens of times, trying to iron the wrinkles out of my otherwise perfect plan. Even the whole Wendy Wood situation didn't change my opinion of my father. Like Thelma said, he was a good man. And I was proud of the way he took the blame for me that night.

Why did he want to take the blame? Because he loves me? Or because he doesn't want me to face the same kind of shame he did back in Vinton?

On the way home, I tried to figure out what Clarence was thinking. His eyes were on the road. He drove carefully and slowly and stopped at every yellow light—I guess he couldn't stand the thought of another run-in with a police officer. He wasn't mad at me—not too mad, anyway. And he wasn't mad at George Penn. It was life he was angry with. Maybe even God. Angry because the color of his skin meant that he had to hold back and not say what he'd really like to. Angry because no matter how hard he worked, or how much he put into life, he knew he would always be seen as a second-rate citizen.

The moon was full, and so bright and big that it was visible over the city lights. I bent my head down so I could see it out the windshield, and Larry followed suit.

He stared at it for a long time, then started whistling again.

"Larry," I said, "Do you mind not whistling? I can't take it."

"Sure." He rolled the window all the way down and rested his elbow on the door. Then—as if he was reading my mind—he started talking about the injustice of the situation. Of course, he put his own spin on it, but I knew what he meant.

"Everything is against you when you're not white," he said quietly.

I saw Clarence's head turn, just a little bit.

"Right," I said.

"Everything is for white people—they've got all the power. Especially white guys. I never thought about it back in Porcupine Plain," said Larry, "but everyone with authority seems to be a white guy. The Mayor's a white guy, the Prime Minister's a white guy, all the police are white guys." He leaned out the window and looked up at the sky. "Even the man in the moon is a white guy."

CHAPTER TEN

Sister Beatrice enjoyed having me come along for the trip. Marsha did not. It was clear that she was only tolerating me because she had to—as one would put up with hay fever, or a bad haircut. I felt the same way about her. Having endured hours of riding in an enclosed vehicle with Marsha, listening to her dirge-like voice blather on about the devil (she called him the Captain of Death), I kept wondering why I had volunteered for this misery. It was like pounding my head with a hammer because it felt so good when I finally stopped. Every time she fell quiet, it was such a blissful relief that if I could have bottled and sold the feeling, it would have been more addictive that Janis's Southern Comfort.

I was, of course, grateful for the ride, even with Marsha, because it allowed me to keep most of my cash should I be lucky enough to be invited to stay in Texas. And it was only one way; I wouldn't have to endure a round trip. Already, our journey south would be 1,500 miles, most of it along US-85. Marsha informed me that we would be traveling a straight line through the Dakotas, Wyoming, Colorado, and New Mexico. I had the distinct feeling that most everything in her life ran along a fairly straight line. The highway continued on as far as El Paso, but my journey (at least with the nuns) would end at Route 66, in Albuquerque.

"I hope you don't mind me bringing my instruments," I said to Sister Beatrice. She was in the backseat, our luggage was in the back of the station wagon, and since it was my turn to drive, I was at the wheel. Marsha was up front, next to me. She didn't appear to have much in the way of luggage, although she had brought a large paper bag full of nuts and seeds.

"Not at all," replied Sister Beatrice, leaning her head back to take a rest. "This car is quite roomy, if nothing else." By that time, we were over the border, and passing through Fortuna, North Dakota. And also by that time, I had heard several of Marsha's sermons. She gave a long, garbled lecture on the Evil One, and how seduction is all around us. I think she was trying to tell me that my going to Austin to meet Janis at Threadgill's was something akin to what happened to Eve in the Garden.

"It was because she was so close to the forbidden tree that Satan could entice her into tasting the deadly fruit. It is his policy to send temptations through hands we do not suspect. Drinking and music make you more susceptible to the lies of the devil."

Steering with one hand, I riffled through the bags beside

me to find the red licorice I'd brought along, and offered a piece to Marsha to shut her up. She and Sister Beatrice each took one, but it didn't have the result that I'd hoped for. Although she chewed on every bite at least a hundred times, she still managed to tell me more about Jesus and more about the consequences of sin, as well as the last judgment, and fishes and vessels, and rewards for the faithful.

It started to pour, which was good, because the sound of the rain combined with the *shhh-shhh-shhh* of the tires on the wet highway and the rhythm of the wipers drowned out Marsha's attempt at exorcising me of my demons. I was soon lulled into a dream-like state where I no longer heard her voice and could think, instead, about my own life. My future as a blues musician.

And Clarence. I started to think about him.

I hated having to leave so soon, especially after what happened at The Beehive. He didn't say anything, but I knew he was upset. I knew he couldn't stand to have another person in his life leave him—first it was Johnny Foster, then Thelma, and now me. Everybody that mattered to him was gone.

But I had no choice. *I had no choice.*

I thought Clarence would be glad that I'd offered to take Johnny's medals down to Amarillo, to Agnes Foster. He'd talked about doing it for years, but never made it back to Texas after Johnny died. I figured that since Albuquerque and Amarillo were both on Route 66, I could hit Agnes's curio shop on my way to Austin. If I didn't have time on the way down, I could go after. To me, it seemed like a good idea.

"Oh, no, I don't...I don't think so," said Clarence. It had been warm the night before, so we were outside on the deck that overlooked the lot behind the garage. He didn't offer any kind of an explanation, just sipped his cola and stared at the stars.

"It's not far from where I'm going."

"Amarillo's nowhere near Austin," he protested. "Five hundred miles anyway." He thought for a minute. "It's up in the panhandle."

"Yeah, but I'll be taking a bus from Albuquerque, and that's on Route 66. Only a few hours to Amarillo." I crushed ice between my teeth. "It's no problem, Clarence. And I'll be super careful with those medals, honest I will."

I could tell from the expression on his face that he wasn't worried about me losing the medals, and he wasn't concerned how far out of my way the trip might take me. No, Clarence didn't want me to go to Agnes Foster's curio shop, and I demanded to know why.

"What's going on, Clarence?" I said. "You've been wanting to get those medals back to Johnny's mother for as long as I can remember."

"I think I will mail them—tomorrow." He nodded his head as if to convince himself. "Yeah. Tomorrow."

"You told me you would never trust those medals to the postal service." I looked him straight in the eye. "What is it, Clarence? Don't you have faith in me?" I couldn't figure out what his problem was, and gave up trying. "Okay, go ahead and mail the damn things." I got up and went back inside.

Then I opened the screen door and yelled to him. "I'll check in with Agnes Foster when I'm down there. Make sure they arrived safely."

"No!" Clarence jumped out of his chair and into the kitchen.

"What's wrong? What is it?"

He took a deep breath, then went to the sink and got himself a glass of water. He splashed some of it onto his face.

"Do whatever you want, Easy. You're eighteen now. You can do whatever you want. I can't stop you."

Can't stop me? What's that supposed to mean?

Just the thought of those war medals got Clarence so bent out of shape, I felt guilty for even mentioning them. I decided to take them with me anyway, since I knew he'd be relieved once Agnes had them in her possession.

It was Sister Beatrice who drew me out of my thoughts, and back to the yellow submarine.

"Why don't you have a rest, Louisiana. Marsha can take over now."

"Please, call me Easy," I said, pulling off to the side of the road to switch places with my Bible-thumping co-pilot.

"Why were you named Louisiana?" asked Marsha, sliding out the car door.

I shifted to the passenger side while she made her way around the station wagon. She smoothed out the front of her jumper, stretched her neck, then took her place at the wheel.

"My parents are from there. From Vinton." I reached over into the seat behind me and grabbed my purse to check for the medals. I'd wrapped them up in a remnant of fabric from Thelma's sewing box, then put them inside a brown envelope.

"Where's Vinton?" asked Sister Beatrice.

"It's a Cajun town," I replied, passing around more licorice. "Down in the bayou." I smiled. "You know, Janis told me that she used to go there all the time. To listen to music."

Marsha started to hum a hymn, as if to drive out any evil forces I might have conjured up by mentioning Janis's name. I gazed out the window and watched North Dakota go by in ribbons of greens and golds, clear and bright against the rainy gray sky and thought back to what Clarence had told me before I'd left.

"Austin isn't Saskatoon," he said, watching me finish the last of my packing. I didn't know if he was trying to talk me out of going, or simply warning me, but he didn't look any too happy about my impending trip.

"I know."

"No, Easy. You don't know. Don't be fooled by all the talk about civil rights. Things are just as bad as ever. Worse even, because the white folks resent us even more."

"I'll be careful."

"You haven't faced racism, Easy—"

"Yes, I have," I argued. "Remember Miss Poultice? And I took a lot of crap in school, too. And what about last night, Clarence? If I'd been a white girl, it wouldn't have happened."

"Everything you've seen, everything you've experienced here in Saskatoon is nothing—nothing like you're gonna see in Texas. A lot of white folks are all right, but a lot of them would like nothing more than to spit in your face, Easy. And the problem is, you can't tell one from the other until it's too late." He opened the door that led downstairs. "Don't forget to tell me when you're leaving," he added.

"Clarence—wait!" I stopped him before he went to work. "I know what you've been through—you and Thelma. She told me about the Negro Motorist Green Book. She told me—"

"Did she tell you what it was like to have to worry about driving through a sunset town—a town where they could arrest a black person simply for *being there* after dark? Did she tell you how humiliating it was to have to carry a guide to tell you what restaurants would accept you and what ones would throw you out?"

"But Clarence," I argued, "they stopped printing that book six years ago."

"I know, Easy. I know." He shook his head back and forth. "But I have a feeling you're gonna wish they hadn't."

♪

"Let's stop for a meal," said Sister Beatrice, and once again my focus was drawn back into the car. The rain was still coming down, but I liked it. It smelled fresh and clean when I let the mist blow in through the window.

By this time, we'd passed through a good chunk of North Dakota, and were almost to the church in Belfield, where we'd be staying the night. The nuns planned on sleeping in a residence nearby; I brought along my sleeping bag and would be roughing it in the pews. But we all agreed that since we'd made better time than expected, it might not be a bad idea to stop for dinner.

It was one of those family restaurants that you find on highways, with dishes already filled with rubbery Jell-O and congealed rice pudding and big thick pies behind glass. You have to point at what you want, and the person serving you never gets it right; so if you want lime Jell-O, you might end up with coconut cream pie. When we came through the door, everyone looked up and smiled reverently when they saw that two of us were nuns. Marsha sucked it all in, and floated a few inches off the ground. I walked stiffly, self-conscious of the fact that they likely reckoned I'd either run away from a mission, or was out on a day pass for good behavior.

I had french fries and a Coke. It was all I could afford on my budget. (As much as I hated to admit it, I had to keep enough money for airfare home, in case things didn't go as expected.) Sister Beatrice and Marsha had big shrimp platters with rolls and salad because the pope was picking up their tab. Marsha left more than half of it, though, so I finished it off.

This was the first meal I'd ever eaten with nuns in my life, and I stupidly forgot about saying grace. So when the waitress put the plate in front of me, I grabbed the ketchup bottle, banged on it a few times, then dove into my food. Marsha pursed her lips, flared her thin nostrils, and gave me "the look." Her eyes blazed, but her voice was unemotional when she finally observed, "We haven't said grace."

"Oh, God. I mean…oh, dear. I'm sorry." I pulled a half-eaten french fry out of my mouth and returned it to my plate.

Then I folded my hands and hung my head.

I'd hoped Sister Beatrice would say the grace, because I figured she'd be much quicker. But she deferred to Marsha, who carried on and on in her woebegone voice, praying so vigorously that it didn't seem like we were giving thanks for our dinner. It was more like we were all in a leaky canoe and could hear the falls just ahead.

Once she'd finished, I returned to my (cold) supper and watched her eat; from the corner of my eye, I followed the progress of each bite. I got to wondering why she wanted to be a nun. What turned her so sour in the first place? It was as if Marsha was encased in glass; there was no getting inside her mind, and that was what made her so boring. So insipid. And despite what I imagined were hundreds and hundreds of hours of long prayers every night on bony knees, I doubted very much that God was too interested in her either.

CHAPTER ELEVEN

I was already thinking that this is what purgatory must be like when Marsha decided to embark on the painstaking process of choosing her new name. After forty-eight hours of travel and seven meals with her, plus two nights tossing and turning on a hard pew with Mother Mary and a choir of angels looking down on me in judgment, I was in no mood to listen. It was Sunday morning, and we were on our way to the western edge of Denver. Sister Beatrice had explained that we would be spending the day at Our Lady of Mount Carmel Convent. I declined, telling her I'd planned on taking in the sights. Actually, I'd planned on doing some busking, but since it was the Sabbath, I wasn't sure if she'd approve. For me, Sunday was the day to do exactly what I would on any other day, but feel guilty doing it.

Sister Beatrice was at the wheel, with Marsha beside her,

FREEDOM'S JUST ANOTHER WORD

and I was fidgeting in the backseat, when old sourpuss got this sudden urge to decide what she'd be called. I gathered from their conversation that when she became a novice and began to wear the full habit, she'd be given a new name by the Mother Superior. She was allowed to make suggestions, and from the sound of it, the church usually went with the choice of the individual. All of this was slated to happen in early October. By then she'd be back in Saskatoon—and, with any luck, I wouldn't.

"What about Ivanna?" she asked Sister Beatrice. "It means God is gracious." Then, in a somber voice, she tried another one. "I could be called Sister Nastasiya."

"What does that mean?" asked Sister Beatrice politely. We were stopped at a red light, otherwise she might not have, and we'd have been spared the pietistic definition.

"It means *of the resurrection*. Isn't that wonderful?"

Sister Beatrice gave a little nod. "So you will be taking a Ukrainian name, then?"

"Perhaps. To reflect my heritage." Although that was the only thing she'd said so far that made any sense to me, I had the feeling that if Marsha looked far enough into that ancestry of hers, she'd find more than lovers of cabbage rolls and perogies. She'd probably turn up a few judges, some jury members, and at least one executioner.

Then she changed her mind. "Maybe I won't take a Ukrainian name. Maybe it should be something universal, like Faith or Hope."

No mention of charity.

103

By the time we'd parked the yellow submarine at the convent, and Marsha had returned to her heritage and finally penciled in her choice—*Bohuslava*, which meant God's glory—I'd decided that it was a good thing to be named after a state. Less pretentious. Nothing to live up to. So while Sister Bohuslava spent the day with her fellow holier-than-thous, I took my accordion to the first park I could find in the hope of attracting a few listeners and maybe some cash.

The Mile High City really is a mile above sea level, and the downtown district, being only a few miles east of the Rocky Mountain foothills, offered such a magnificent view, I wished I had a camera so I could take some shots to show Clarence and Larry. In fact, the mountains, visible in all of their snow-topped magnificence, looked just like mountains should. Against the backdrop of a cerulean sky, they offered such spectacular scenery that I almost hated to leave. Almost, but not quite, because even though Austin probably wouldn't present itself quite as dramatically as Denver, it'd still have Janis Joplin in it.

I'd barely started playing my accordion when a group of girls approached me and told me to stop.

"I will not."

"Yes, you will, you disgusting—" She used the *n* word, but Thelma always told me that if anyone ever addressed me in so vile a way, I must erase it from my mind, like I'd never heard it in the first place.

There were five of them. All of them were white. All but one of them were blonde, and she was a brunette with a temper. She tried to pull the frottoir off my neck.

"What an ugly thing it is," she hissed, tugging at the strap and almost choking me to death in the process.

"Leave me alone!" I protested. "I'm not bothering you or anyone else. Mind your own—"

"You horrible, smelly, dirty—" She used that word again. *Smelly? I hadn't had a bath for a couple of days, but my clothes were clean. Smelly?*

Two older women walked past carrying parcels. They watched as the gang of girls circled me, but they didn't offer any help. They ignored the situation and went on their way.

I was scared, but figured the best approach was to do nothing, and maybe they'd leave. It turned out to be the worst approach. Some guys—boyfriends of theirs—joined them. The biggest one, who looked like a football player, proudly sported a KKK symbol on his shirt, and the look in his eye told me that if I didn't get out of *their* park voluntarily, he'd see to it that I did. Feet first.

I pushed my accordion around to the front of my chest and was about to bolt, when I remembered something else Thelma said.

If you meet up with bigots, Easy, you must protect yourself and walk away. But never run. Never run.

So I walked away. They continued to put me down—their slurs hitting me in the back like arrows—but I kept going. Through the park. Back to the yellow submarine. Back to the safety of the convent. Back to Marsha, even if I'd have to admit to conducting business on a Sunday. Maybe that was why this happened to me. I went around the back of the convent to where the nuns were all having tea in the garden and found Sister Beatrice first.

"I never thought it would happen in Denver," I said.

"What is it? What happened?"

"I knew that I'd have to face it in the deep South—"

"Face what?"

"Did you know the Ku Klux Klan was here in Denver?" I asked her.

She turned down her mouth and nodded. "I did. They've been gunning for us Catholics too." She put an arm around my back. "Tell me what they did to you, Louisiana."

She sat me down and brought me something to drink. Marsha was still trying out Bohuslava on the other Sisters, but when she finally joined us, and listened to my story, her face actually softened a bit. I detected a small but definite chink in her armor.

She didn't say a word. In fact, it was almost as if she couldn't say a word. As if she didn't know how to show emotion, or relate to my pain. Instead of giving me a hug, or reminding me that people like those girls are sickos with problems of their own, or screaming out loud about the injustices of the world, she stood in stony silence. And by the time she did say something, she'd managed to replace that one brick I'd knocked from the wall around her heart.

"I will pray for you," she said solemnly.

"Pray for me?"

"I'll pray that it doesn't happen again."

Gee, thanks, Marsha. That ought to help.

Luckily, Sister Beatrice decided to cut her stay at the convent short and get back on the road the next morning. And while I was wise enough to realize that the jerks I'd had the misfortune of meeting in the park were not a representative sample of the otherwise decent citizens of Denver, I was still relieved when we finally crossed the state line, and left "Kolorado" behind us forever.

♫

I'd heard a lot about Route 66, not only the stories about Johnny Foster's mother and her curio shop, but also reminiscences from people I'd met who had traveled it from end to end. I'd read Steinbeck's *Grapes of Wrath* in high school, about the dust bowl in the 1930s and the farm workers that went west to California in search of work. And I knew from Clarence that the towns along Route 66 would soon be bypassed by the new Interstate highway.

What I didn't know was how emotionally attached so many people were to this stretch of asphalt. I was in a diner near Albuquerque when I realized how critical the situation really was. It was late Wednesday afternoon, and we were almost to the junction of Routes 85 and 66. We were tired and hungry and wanted something to eat before we made our way to the nuns' final destination, the Sisters of Charity Convent.

A big-boned waitress gave the oilcloth on our table a swipe with her rag, then came back with water and menus. The nuns ordered their usual feasts; I settled for the cheapest thing I could find. I remembered to wait to say grace, and when Marsha couldn't finish what was on her plate, I polished it off. This tactic had been working well across five states. By my calculations, the pope had saved me at least twenty bucks. The three of us were saying our good-byes, or in Marsha's case, our good-riddances, since I planned on taking the next bus to Amarillo. From there, after I'd given the medals to Agnes Foster, I'd be on my way to Threadgill's. On my way to a new life.

"I think you should stay over at the convent, Louisiana," said Sister Beatrice. "It's too dangerous to travel alone at night." She checked her watch. "It's at least four hours to Amarillo. And it's already past six."

I waited for Marsha to agree with her, but she adjusted the bobby pins in that stupid white veil of hers and said nothing.

"If there's a bus tonight," I said, "I'll be on it." The thought of sleeping one more night in another gloomy institution, with the faint whispers of prayers leaking from tiny cracks under closed doors, made a mortuary seem more inviting. But not wanting to seem like an ingrate, I did thank the nuns for letting me ride with them. We settled up the gas bill, and while they finished their coffee, I bought a postcard and moved to an empty booth to fill it out. It was the perfect one to send to my father, because it had a Phillips 66 service station on the front.

Dear Clarence and Larry (and Mrs. Hill because I know you're reading this.) I am writing from a roadside diner near Albuquerque. Am doing well and hope you are too. I'm on my way to Amarillo next— hope you're not mad that I took the medals, Clarence. Pet Gillie for me. Love, Easy.

As I was addressing the card, I overheard a conversation between two men in the booth across from me. A beer-bellied trucker was working a toothpick between his molars, talking to a sad-looking man with sideburns about his rig. He pointed to it, and since it was parked near the window, I could see the bumper sticker which read *Everything is Bigger in Texas.* At first I thought they were talking about someone's death because they kept mentioning the fifteenth of November, 1968.

"Yeah, that was it. Right there," said the one with the belly. "End of it all."

"Fine for those suits in the capital. Fine for the politicians, too," declared the other one. "But that old road means life." He had tears in his eyes. "Goddam super slab! It's gonna kill every business from Chicago to Los Angeles. Every goddam business." He wiped his eye with a serviette. "It's gonna kill me too."

I listened for a while, and it turned out that November 15, 1968 was the day they opened the I-40 and diverted every bit of traffic off the mother road. The businesses that had built up over the years on Route 66 would soon be nothing but bare lots and the occasional tumbleweed rolling past. I thought for a minute about change, and how some things were changing for the better—six years before, I'd have needed the Negro Motorist Green Book to determine if I could eat in that diner—but not all change was good.

I listened as the trucker read a newspaper article out loud to his friend. It read like an obituary.

The most famous highway in the world. The Mother Road. America's Main Street. Call it what you like, that string of neon lights, motor courts, diners and cafés is like no other place in the world.

Route 66 is tourist traps and speed traps. Fly traps dangling over Arborite tables that are stickier than they are, and seats that never get a chance to cool off. Porch swings, treacherous curves with crosses in the weeds to prove it, and fry cooks serving up more grease than the service stations. It's the Painted Desert and the Petrified Forest. It's dreamers and drifters and the waitress who can sling coffee, crack eggs, and find out where those drifters are from and where they're headed, all before the toast pops. It's two thousand miles of concrete and asphalt and mustard and maple syrup and a million lights sputtering out Good Eats, Clean Rooms, *and* Jesus Loves You.

And by the time we ring in 1971, it will be gone forever.

The man wiped his eyes again, and I thought about what he'd just read. I wondered if Janis had taken Route 66 when she moved from Texas to California, and what was going through her mind at the time—when she was nobody. When she was just another one of those dreamers and drifters.

"I wish the bus would take Route 66, not the Interstate," I told Sister Beatrice, once I was back in their booth. "I want to see more of it—before it disappears." I licked a stamp and put it on the back of my postcard. "Before it's gone for good."

"Efficiency is what matters," mumbled Marsha, sounding more like a foreman than a nun.

Sister Beatrice handed me a bus schedule she'd obtained from the waitress, and happily pointed out that I'd missed the last one out of town. "You'll have to stay with us at the convent!"

I checked the pamphlet and noticed, to my dismay, that the coach used the new Interstate to make the trip from Albuquerque to Amarillo. Listening to those truck drivers made me all the more determined to follow Route 66, even if it meant hitchhiking. I waited a minute, and sure enough, Thelma appeared in my thoughts.

You'll get yourself killed, Easy.

"I'll be careful...."

"Pardon me?" said Sister Beatrice.

"I was talking to myself." I smiled. "I was talking to Thelma, actually."

"Who's Thelma?" asked Sister Beatrice.

"My mother. Well, not my real mother. The mother who raised me."

I felt the full impact of Marsha's granite eyes. "You were adopted?"

"It's a long story," I said. Then I changed the subject. Having decided to take a middle position—I would hitch a ride down the Mother Road, but wait until daylight to do it—I told Sister Beatrice that I would accept her offer to stay the night at the convent.

As it turned out, it was a good thing I did.

CHAPTER TWELVE

Sister Beatrice had to make another stop, to visit a priest she knew on the outskirts of Albuquerque, so it was late by the time we arrived at the convent. It was located near Central Avenue, which is what Route 66 was called within the city limits. We drove past countless motor courts and tacky little stores that stayed open to catch the last dribble of trade; colorful ribbons of neon outlined roadside cafes and honky-tonk bars.

The convent itself was a huge, adobe structure that sat quietly on a side street, watching the comings and goings of the citizens of Albuquerque, much like the river did in Saskatoon. It didn't seem to pass judgment, although it served as a reminder that all of this—the noise, the crowds, the hullabaloo—was temporal. Not eternal like God. A single star twinkled in the night sky behind the cross on the roof, and somehow the place reminded me of a Christmas card. Thelma's cards were always like that: the desert, the star, the white buildings. Bethlehem.

Sister Beatrice said the convent was Pueblo Revival architecture, and told me the history of the mission, while Marsha examined her fingernails for dirt. It was an inviting place, not at all like the forbidding convents we'd been staying in. And although in New Mexico the days are hot, the nights can be quite cool; the convent, though, was warm and friendly. Despite the late hour, Marsha hurried off to find the Mother Superior, and Sister Beatrice exited with nuns, leaving me to bed down either in the sanctuary or next door in the mission building.

I chose the latter, and found it full of people.

The place was designed so that males and females had separate sleeping quarters, but shared an area in the middle for eating and socializing. It was almost eleven by that time, but a nun was sitting in the middle of the room, and around her were fifteen or sixteen young men and women. They all had that same foggy look that Janis had. Like their station wasn't quite tuned in.

"Come here, honey," the nun said, passing me a plate of cookies. "They're not too stale," she added, her mouth full. Obviously not the fussy type, it was apparent that she was happy to eat the same food as those who had no choice. "Coffee and tea over there." She gestured to a table against the wall.

The guy next to me was completely strung out, but clearheaded enough to realize that I was new. He tried to hand me a vanilla wafer.

"No, thanks, really."

"They're better than usual," he assured me.

"Past the best-before date?" I asked.

"Yeah, but you can't tell."

Wanting to get an early start the next morning, I thought I'd turn in and asked the nun if I could have a bed.

"Help yourself," she said, pointing to the women's area. "We won't be much longer. We're having a couple more songs first." She got up, walked across the room, and picked up a guitar.

"Songs?"

"Sure, songs." She took her place in the middle again.

"Mind if I join in? I'll get my accordion!"

"Wonderful."

I ran out to the yellow submarine, and from outside could hear them start into the Jackie DeShannon song "Put a Little Love in Your Heart." Not the blues, but a good one nevertheless. I hurried back and joined in. The way the nun played guitar and sang, she reminded me of Maria in *The Sound of Music*. We did a few more numbers—all pop songs that you wouldn't expect a nun to know—then everyone started washing cups and plates and putting things into cupboards. By their clothes, I could tell that these young people didn't have a penny to their name; they were lucky, though, to have such a joyful place to spend time and eat and sleep.

"You have a marvelous voice," the nun said, jamming her guitar back into its case.

"Thanks. I'm on my way to Texas…um…to become a blues singer."

"No way!" she said. "Well, good luck with that. Drop by sometime and let me know how it goes, will you?"

The nun sounded like she really meant it.

"What's your name, anyway?" she asked.

"I'm Louisiana Merritt. But everyone calls me Easy."

"Okay, Easy, why Texas? Why not Louisiana, like your name? That's the place for blues, isn't it?" She grabbed a tea towel and started drying mugs, so I followed suit.

"You won't believe it but—"

"I'll believe it."

"I met Janis Joplin—up in Saskatoon, where I'm from. And she invited me to Texas to play for people she knows." Just as I spoke those words, I felt a cold, bony hand grab the back of my arm. I jumped backwards and turned, expecting to see Boris Karloff standing behind me.

It was Marsha.

"The Mother Superior doesn't want to hear about a drug-addicted sinner like Janis Joplin, I'm sure," she declared, her lips stretched tight with disapproval.

"Mother Superior?" I asked. I'd always thought a Mother Superior was a gray-haired old woman with an office—like a businessman, only in a habit.

"Yes—I'm sorry, Easy. I'm Reverend Mother Grace. I didn't have a chance—"

"No, *I'm* sorry, Reverend Mother," said Marsha. "She shouldn't bring up that woman's name in your presence."

"Why not?" asked the nun. "I love Janis Joplin." She turned to me. "That's an amazing opportunity for you. I hope it works out."

"You…*love*…that woman?" Marsha abhorred Janis and enjoyed doing it. "She's helping to destroy our nation. She promotes drug use and alcoholism and…well, everyone knows she's a prostitute."

"Prostitute?"

"Well, she might as well be, the way she—" She stopped once it finally dawned on her that Mother Grace wasn't on her side.

The older nun took a good long look at Marsha. "So you must be the postulant from Saskatoon I've heard so much about."

Somebody must have warned her.

"Yes. I tried to find your office the minute I arrived."

"I'm out here most of the time," she said with a smile.

Marsha gave me the evil eye, as if she'd discovered me trying to convert the Reverend Mother to atheism. I left the two of them to get acquainted, and walked around the room. One guy had collected a small group around himself and was insisting they do something to stop the dirty capitalists in government. He was determined that everyone hear "the truth," and I guessed that this was nothing new for him; he'd probably been one of those kids who assembled the neighborhood children to tell them where babies came from.

While he rattled on, most of the others went into the respective sleeping areas. That was when I noticed a guy sitting alone on the floor, his back resting against the wall. He was twenty or so and would have been downright handsome, but his hair was filthy, and his clothes were full of gaping holes. Beside him on the floor was a bag of stale cookies that the nun had given him to take home, although I doubted he had one to go back to.

His gaze was so firmly fixed on the ground, I figured there was no point in trying to strike up a conversation. I returned to Reverend Mother Grace and Marsha, who was still expressing her opinions about Janis Joplin and the modern western world in general.

I stood there listening, and waited to see how the Mother Superior would handle the situation—how she'd go about lowering Marsha's nose a notch. I was a Sunday-school dropout, but even I knew that Jesus himself forgave prostitutes and other assorted sinners. Why couldn't Marsha? Not that I thought Janis needed anybody's forgiveness. She was amazing. And what blues singer didn't have issues? Both Bessie Smith and Billie Holiday drank to excess, and Billie Holiday fought a heroin addiction her entire life. Both were accused of reckless behavior. Both were considered prostitutes. Both were spontaneous and emotional singers who turned their tragic lives into moving music. What right did stupid Marsha have to judge Janis Joplin?

"What do you know about Mother d'Youville, Marsha?" asked the older nun. I was hoping she was going to tell her off for going over Jesus' head and not forgiving anybody; instead she gave her a history lesson on the Grey Nuns of Montreal and the woman who started the order.

"I know they began in Quebec in the 1700s, and I know they worked tirelessly to help the sick." Marsha thought for a minute. "And then they went to the west of Canada to build hospitals."

I fought back a yawn while Marsha tried to remember more. Thankfully, she couldn't.

"It's late, so I'll make it quick, Marsha," said the Reverend Mother. "The gray habit that you will be wearing once you take your vows is because of a drunk."

Marsha raised her eyebrows.

"Yes, a drunk. You see, Mother d'Youville was married to a notorious bootlegger, and after he died, she founded the order. She and her followers were taunted as *les grises*, which in French means 'the gray women' or 'the drunken women.' She accepted this and wore gray as a constant reminder of her humble origins as the wife of a criminal."

"Why?" I asked.

"By wearing that color every day, it meant she would never forget that she was no better than the people she served."

I nodded, Marsha bit her tongue, and the nun continued talking. "That woman took in the most destitute people and offered them love." She put an arm around the postulant. "Humility isn't an abstract virtue, Marsha. It's an absolute necessity if you plan on mission work. You can't expect to help anyone in this world if you're up on a cloud somewhere."

Marsha said nothing. She just stood there—so straight and so stiff, you'd think she was an exclamation point.

"Mother Grace?" I said.

"Yes, Easy?"

"Who is that young man sitting against the wall? Does he live here?"

"At times," she said. She began picking up paper napkins

from dirty plates and tossing them into a garbage bag. "Roy's a drug addict. Has been for several years now. We've been helping him here at the mission. Once he was clean for three months and was able to work." She stopped. "But the addiction is bigger than he is, I'm afraid. He needs more help than I can give him." She glanced at him. "But I won't stop trying."

"Can't he go to a clinic or something?" sniffed Marsha. She avoided making eye contact with the guy completely.

"He could, but that would be like death to him. No music, no life. No, I need to keep him here. That's his only hope," she explained. "I know there's an answer for Roy. I just need a bit more time to find it."

While Marsha scurried to assist Mother Grace with the clean up, I decided to talk to Roy after all.

"Hi," was the most brilliant thing I could come up with.

"Yeah," he said.

"I'm Louisiana, but everyone calls me Easy. I'm from Canada. From Saskatoon." I felt like I was talking to myself. "Saskatchewan," I added as an afterthought.

He raised his head, but his eyes looked past me. His face was flushed, his pupils were dilated, and he was sweating more than he should have been.

You hear all the time about people who shoot drugs, but who function as teachers and doctors and judges and live "normal lives" as members of society, because they handle the drugs so well. Roy was not one of those people; his eyes were on two different circuits. He could look at you with one, while watching someone else with the other.

"There's no one can pull me back in," he mumbled.

"Pull you back in?"

"Can *you* pull me back in?" He reached for my arm and tugged, but I didn't know what to do, so he let go.

Mother Grace and Marsha came to tell us it was time for lights out.

"You can stay where you are, Roy," she added. "But there is a clean bed if you want it."

He didn't answer her, and grabbed my arm again instead. I tried to break free, but the Mother Superior gave me a look that meant *Let him hold your arm. He needs to hold your arm.*

"You're going to Woodstock to see Janis Joplin. I heard you say that." His eyes were still out of focus, so it felt weird answering him.

"No, I'm not."

"I heard you say you're meeting Janis Joplin. Can I come to Yasgur's Farm with you?" he asked.

"Uh…I…I'm not going to Woodstock. I'm going to Austin to meet her. She's going to help my singing career. I hope."

Roy said nothing for a full minute, but never let go of my arm.

"Janis Joplin, she could do it," he said. "She could pull me back in. Could I hold her arm?"

"Do what?" Marsha grumbled.

"Hold Janis Joplin's arm."

Mine was starting to get pins and needles in it, but I didn't move.

"And how would that help you?" asked the Mother Superior.

120

"She's been down. She's been down, I can tell by the way she sings." He dropped his head, then pulled it up again. "Can I come with you to Yasgur's Farm?"

"Woodstock was last year, Roy." Mother Grace wiped her eye with a napkin; I could see that she was truly concerned for Roy and didn't know what to do. Then she turned off the lights, and once Marsha and I came through, she shut the door behind us.

"You're staying in there, aren't you?" asked Marsha, intimating that I was suited more for the mission than the convent.

"Yes, I just want to put my accordion back in the car."

Mother Grace looked up at the sky, then at me, then at Marsha, like she was trying to figure something out. Finally, she told us what was on her mind, and I don't know which one of us was more shocked, Marsha or me.

"I've made a decision on your placement, Marsha," she said, this time with a stern voice, quite unlike the one she'd been using in the mission.

"You have?" Marsha beamed, but not for long.

"If Easy will agree to it, I'd like you to go to Austin and meet Janis Joplin. That's what I want you to do."

"I don't know if I can take anyone with me," I protested.

"I assume the bar is open to the public," declared the Mother Superior. "I realize that I am asking a lot of you, but—"

"Please, Reverend Mother," begged Marsha. "Anything but that. *Anything*. I don't like the woman and I don't want to meet her."

"My mind's made up," she said. "Easy, if you will take

Marsha with you, we could help with your expenses. We don't have much in the way of money, but I'm sure Sister Beatrice will let you take the station wagon, and you could stay with our sisters in Austin."

"But I have to go to Amarillo first. I'm delivering something to a friend there. For my father."

"Fine. You can stay at St. Michael's Parish. It's on the road between Amarillo and Austin. I have good friends there."

This woman has friends everywhere, I thought.

"No, *please*, Reverend Mother. I'd rather stay here and learn from you," cried Marsha.

"Since you find so many things wrong with Janis Joplin, I think she's the one to teach you about people. And drug addiction." She set her jaw. "My job is to train you to do mission work, and I think that meeting her will do more than I ever could. It's very easy to see the dark side of drugs—any fool can do that. But until you find out what attracts young people to them in the first place, you will never be able to help anyone."

"But—"

"I've made my decision. And there's one other thing—I want you to take Roy along."

Marsha said nothing, but had an expression on her face that if audible would have been something like: *you can put red-hot nails in my eyeballs but I'll never do it.*

"Roy's tried to kill himself twice. Next time, he might be successful. Maybe if he met Janis Joplin, talked to her, and held on to her arm…" She bit her bottom lip. "The boy is desperate. Please take him."

I didn't know how to respond, but Marsha did.

"Maybe if you threatened him. Told him he couldn't stay at the mission unless he quit doing drugs. That would make him stop."

"No," said Mother Grace. "Absolutely not. This is the one place he can come without judgment. No demands. The world is enough of a threat for Roy. This is God's house, Marsha. God's house accepts everyone, no questions asked." She turned and went back to the convent.

"What about Sister Beatrice?" hollered Marsha. "I'm supposed to stay with her."

The Reverend Mother kept walking. "She'll be here when you get back," she said.

Marsha waited for the door to close behind the nun, then gave it to me straight. "I might have to go to Austin with you, but I will not set one foot in that bar. Not one foot. And there's no way I'm taking Roy. I refuse to travel with a drug addict. It goes against my principles, and I will not do it."

CHAPTER THIRTEEN

It wasn't long after seven that I awoke to the squeals of children and the crack of a bat hitting a baseball. From the window beside my bed, I saw Mother Grace and a bunch of children in a nearby field; it was obviously a team practice, since she was banging balls into the air for them to catch. A battered old school bus was parked nearby, so I figured they'd soon be on their way to a game.

I got dressed and headed out the back door, into the grassy area behind the convent. The rising sun stained the eastern sky like spilled salsa, and I could already feel the heat of the day building. In Saskatoon, it would have taken until noon. I got to thinking about the garage and wondered how Larry and Clarence and Gillie were doing. Maybe it was because I was so far from home, or maybe it was all that talk of prostitutes the night before, but I started thinking about that god-awful

Wendy Wood again too. I detested thinking about her, and while I was normally quite successful when it came to erasing her from my mind, I'd spent the entire night hating her and wondering how—how could Clarence have been attracted to such a woman? Didn't he love Thelma enough to resist? He did love Thelma—I knew that—so why did he do it?

My thoughts were interrupted when two nuns whisked past me with a small ladder and headed to the bus. One held the ladder while the other threw up the hood. She studied the engine for a long while. The confused look on her face reminded me of Thelma when she decided to learn a bit about auto parts so she could help us in the garage. It was a hopeless cause and we had laughed about it many times thereafter.

God, I miss you, Thelma.

You help those women with their bus, Easy, she told me, so I did.

"Anything I can do?" I asked the nun with the ladder.

"I hope so. Do you know about engines?"

"Do you?" asked the one under the hood. "Mother Grace is supposed to take the team to Santa Rosa, and the bus won't start. Do you know anything about these things?" She came down the ladder, and the other nun handed her a rag to wipe the grease off her hands.

"I'm a mechanic," I said triumphantly. "Let me take a look."

I quickly realized that the bus was badly in need of new spark plugs and a general overhaul. I checked the oil too, and it was dirty. It hadn't been changed in a year or more.

"When's the last time you had the bus serviced?" I asked. Both nuns shrugged, which told me my suspicions were correct.

"Will it go, Easy?" yelled Mother Grace, surrounded by a team of young ball players. "I couldn't get it started this morning. Can you fix it?"

I found a loose ignition wire, and was able to connect it without tools, and I managed to clean out the intake ports. One of the nuns started up the engine and all the kids cheered. Unfortunately, there wasn't much to cheer about.

"Listen," I said, "this bus needs a lot of work. You might get to Santa Rosa, but there's a good chance you won't get back. Those plugs are in bad shape." I felt guilty for not taking time to fix it for them, but I would have needed a crescent wrench and pliers and more time, not to mention spark plugs and maybe an ignition coil. I couldn't risk delaying my trip to Austin any longer, and Mother Grace knew it. It made me feel selfish, but damn it all, this was the chance of a lifetime.

"You can't keep Janis waiting," she said with a wink. "We're expecting some used parts to come in as donations. And we'll get to a garage once our budget allows for it."

That really made me feel guilty. (Even guiltier than I did for sponging all those meals off the pope.)

The kids piled into the bus, then hung out the windows and cheered again. The two nuns did too. I really wished they hadn't, since those young faces beaming at me made me feel like a self-serving creep.

The Reverend Mother drove. I hoped they all prayed because they were going to need divine help. I couldn't see the terminals on the coil without taking everything apart, but from experience I knew that once the wires start getting loose like that, it's time to replace everything. I would have done it for them, but she was right—I had to get to Austin by Friday, and I wasn't about to let anything, or anybody, get in my way.

Part of me—the part generated by Wendy Wood—wanted to take off right there and then and hitchhike my way to Amarillo. I wished that the Mother Superior had not asked me to take Marsha; traveling with her was the equivalent of attending a hundred funerals. And I wasn't sure how well Roy would travel, either.

But I liked Mother Grace, and didn't want to disappoint her, even if Marsha had no intention of meeting Janis Joplin. Frankly, I was glad, because I didn't want anything to stand in the way of my success. A postulant hanging around would have put a damper on the whole thing. So if it meant traveling with Marsha to Austin, I'd have to put up with it; at least I could save a few more bucks. Up to now, the trip had cost me next to nothing, so I had lots of cash ready, should Janis ask me to come with her to Los Angeles. Or New York. Or the moon. I crossed my fingers, loaded my stuff into the car, and called for Marsha. She appeared from behind a tall cactus, and was as pale as a cadaver.

"Hurry, let's go," she said, looking over her shoulder, like we'd just robbed a bank and the yellow submarine was our getaway car.

"Where's Roy?"

"I can't find him, and we don't have time to search for him, so let's just go, okay?"

"You mean you don't *want* to find him, Marsha," I said. "That's not very postulant-ish of you, is it?"

"He's gone. He's nowhere to be found. Let's get a move on."

♪

"She dresses like a prostitute, she talks like a prostitute, and lives her life like a prostitute," mumbled Marsha from the passenger seat, still seething from having to make the trip to Austin.

"You weren't exactly born in a manger, you know," I said. *Not that we know of, anyway.*

Marsha didn't reply, so I gave it to her. "I don't think it was right for us to leave without Roy. Mother Grace asked you to take him."

"Why should I?" she snapped. "I've spent my entire life trying to stand for something other than drugs and alcohol and iniquity."

"I dunno—I thought this was supposed to be your chosen line of work. Helping people. Helping drug addicts." I shook my head.

"I have chosen to be a nun, and must go where I am told. Things will change. I won't have to work with addicts forever."

"I still think you should have tried to help Roy. He's desperate."

I said no more, and kept on driving, intending to stay at the wheel for the full four-hour drive to Amarillo. That way I could make time when there was nothing to see, and slow down when I wanted to take in the sights along Route 66. We'd already made our way through the twists and turns of Tijeras Canyon, past innumerable white concrete buildings advertising Mexican dishes, the classic *turista* types standing in front, smiling for a camera.

"I can't eat anything Mexican," protested Marsha, when I suggested stopping for lunch at the Casa Grande Diner in Tucumcari. "I'll have heartburn for the rest of the day." While it was good to know she had a heart in there someplace, I was nevertheless determined to sample the tacos and other spicy foods that I'd heard so much about. So while I went inside and had lunch, Marsha waited in the car, sulking like she did at the used-car dealership.

The Casa Grande was not only a tourist stop, but also a gathering place for the locals, and when I sat down at the counter, I noticed immediately that the conversation going on beside me was the same one I'd heard at the last diner: Route 66 and what the building of the Interstate highway was going to do to the Mother Road. Despite the grinding beat of Sly and the Family Stone singing *Thank You (Falettinme Be Mice Elf Again)*—a song that beckons you to stand up and dance— everyone in the place had sober faces, and kept pointing at the road and shaking their heads.

The midday sun was starting to bake the concrete outside; Marsha had finally succumbed to the heat inside the station wagon, and had planted herself against a big elm tree with a girth the size of four men. The bark was covered with the dried skeletons of locusts that had shed their skins.

"That girl's going to get those bug bodies in her hair," said a man near me, looking out at the postulant.

I laughed under my breath.

"It'll do her good," I said.

"She's your friend?" he asked.

"Not really," I said. "Just a traveling companion."

Unfortunately, one of the waitresses switched the radio to a country and western station, which meant nothing but songs about lost love, bad luck, and railroads. It also meant turning my thoughts to Larry, and I began to wonder how everyone was doing back home. I picked out another postcard—this one had a map of the Mother Road on it, with a star that said *You are here, in Tucumcari.* On it I wrote:

> *Hello everyone,*
> *I'm on the road to Amarillo and expect to be*
> *there in a couple hours. Don't worry, the medals*
> *are safe. I'll write again after I see Janis!*
> *Once I come down to earth.*
> *Love, Easy*

While I wrote my message, the guy to my left watched. He did try to look away, but the seats were so close together, he'd have to cover his eyes or go to the washroom again if he wanted to avoid reading what I'd written. I decided to give the guy a break.

"It's just a note for Clarence and Larry back home in Saskatoon," I told him.

"Your family?" he asked, after a couple of swallows of black coffee.

"Clarence is my father. And Larry's from Porcupine Plain," I added as an afterthought.

"Where the hell's that?" asked a man seated to my right.

"Saskatchewan," I said.

"I've been to Saskatoon a few times, making sales," he said, "but never heard of Porcupine Plain." He clunked down his mug. "Good people in Saskatchewan."

"Never been there," said the first guy. "Hear it's cold. Lots of wheat."

"Saskatoon's all right," I said, "but there aren't too many opportunities for a singer like myself."

"Country singer?" asked one of them.

"Blues singer," I replied. "At least, I will be soon. Up to now, I've been working for my father as a mechanic."

"Your father has a garage up there?"

"Yeah. We do regular stuff, but he specializes in classic cars."

"I've got a Model-T back home in Chattanooga," said the salesman. "I'm fixing it up. Gonna be a beauty."

"Bring it up the next time you come to Saskatoon, take it to Merritt garage and ask for Clarence," I said. "He's got parts for Model-T's that you can't find anywhere else. Side windows, caps, stuff like that."

"I will, I will."

"Too bad about Route 66," I said, and they both nodded in agreement.

Then the guy on my left chuckled. "Canadians all say *Root* 66."

"Americans all say *Rowt* 66," I replied.

I realized at that point that although the two men had been quite amiable, the waitress hadn't said a word the entire time. Just stood there, chewing her gum. It went through my head that maybe she didn't approve of a black girl sitting at the counter.

That's just Denver talking. Put it out of your mind.

"Interstate just ain't the same. No friendly faces, no history, no nothing," said one of the men.

I stood up, and fished for money in my pocket. "I'm taking Route 66 to Amarillo. I've got to drop off some war medals for my father." I said good-bye, then paid the waitress. She mumbled, "Good day," but didn't really mean it. Maybe she was racist, maybe she was simply a quiet person.

I guess I'll never know.

"Was your father in the war?" asked the salesman as I was leaving.

"Yeah. On a ship. But the medals were awarded to a friend of his who died. I'm taking them to his mother." I was going to mention the fact that he was one of the first black men to ever be awarded the honor but declined, thanks to my new-found paranoia about racism. I wasn't as self-conscious back in Saskatoon, even after what Miss Poultice and George Penn put me through. Now I was.

I asked the waitress if there was a mailbox nearby, and she gave me some vague instructions about a box next to the Reptile

Ranch down the road. Since I wasn't too fond of poisonous rattlesnakes, I jammed the card into my purse and figured on mailing it later.

I took a cold drink out to Marsha. She said grace, took a tiny disinterested sip, then got back into the car; I returned to driving, minding my own business and trying to enjoy the trip. When we crossed from Quay County, New Mexico into Deaf Smith County, Texas, (and lost an hour, moving instantly from Mountain to Central Time) the sun disappeared, and there was a taut stillness in the air; it was about to storm. Curtains in motels and motor courts were poised in the middle of a sway, half in and half out of the window, and the trees were bent, listening for the sound of the rain to begin.

Clarence always said that the country's so flat in the Texas Panhandle, you can see for two days. He was right. And everything he told me about Route 66 was right, too—friendly little geraniums-in-the-window type of towns like Glenrio and Vega, with their barbershops and soda fountains and cafés surrounded by pickup trucks and Texas-style sedans. Now, of course, all the businesses had signs out front that read *Save Route 66*. And while I agreed that the Interstate was nothing but a passionless slab of monotony, I figured these folks had about as much chance of saving their road as Mother Grace had of saving Roy.

"Most of the people 'round here live and work right on the highway," said the grizzled man who filled our tank. His straw hat was stained with sweat, and rain rolled off the rim and over the side as he made change for a five-dollar bill. "Gonna be right quiet when the rest of the Interstate is paved," he told us, but by the time we'd pulled into his station, we'd passed so many boarded-up diners and broken-hearted movie houses, we could see that the inevitable had already begun.

It took two hundred miles for Marsha to finish eating a handful of nuts and seeds. What she saw in them, I had no idea; during the entire trip south from Saskatoon she had an endless supply. Despite the fact that she ate nonstop, the bag never seemed to go down. That champing of hers got on my nerves, and every fifty miles or so, when I'd stop to unclench my hands from the wheel, I resisted the urge to grab on to her feet and shake her up and down, so I'd be rid of them once and for all.

I noticed too, how she always turned up the radio whenever they were broadcasting bad news. After she'd almost put me to sleep with her usual speech about sin and the Captain of Death, she moved on to bad weather around the world—cyclones, floods—and how they were caused by something she called the hubris of humankind, which turned out to mean pride.

The four-hour drive felt like twenty, but we eventually hit Amarillo, a once-bustling city that now, thanks to the bypass, was nothing but a cluster of beer joints and trailer parks, clinging to the Mother Road and fighting for the attention of every passerby. My eye caught a huge neon sign for the Buckaroo Motel, but Marsha quickly reminded me that we'd be staying in a small parish church on the outskirts of the city. Not the Buckaroo. Too bad, since I imagined a place like that had plenty of stories to tell about its visitors; people who'd driven from Chicago to Santa Monica and the characters they'd met along the way.

It had stopped raining by the time I found the Wagon Wheel Curio Shop. It was a two-room frame building, and I figured Agnes Foster must live in the back because an old umbrella, table, and chairs were huddled beneath a small, weary-looking tree. Another structure, an oversized metal shed, had a huge sign across the front that read FIREWORKS. The paint was chipped and faded, but an outline of the letters was still visible.

Marsha waited in the car while I went inside with the medals. There were no customers, just a woman I assumed was Agnes, sitting behind a counter. The place was cluttered with key chains and glasses and maps and flags—all that Don't-Mess-with-Texas stuff that we had so much of at home. She was smoking a cigarette and drinking a beer, and with a voice that was hoarse enough to be bronchitis, said, "I've got a special on T-shirts. Today only." She pointed to a rack; the shirts were printed with a map of the Lone Star State, and every one of them was coated with a half inch of dust.

Agnes had piercing black eyes and a large bust, and sat directly in front of a creaky old metal fan that blew the smoke from her cigarette around the room. It did nothing to alleviate the heat, however, which was probably why she wore a sleeveless flowered dress that left little to the imagination.

"Mrs. Foster?" I said.

"You know me, child?"

"Yes." I took a deep (and for some reason, quivering) breath. "My name is Louisiana Merritt, and I've brought your son Johnny's war medals all the way from Saskatoon."

She exhaled slowly. Then she stamped out her cigarette into an ashtray that was so full of butts she could barely find room for one more. When she did, the wrinkly flesh that hung from her upper arm wiggled like jelly.

"God help me now," was all she said.

CHAPTER FOURTEEN

Thinking Agnes must be shocked from hearing someone mention her dead son, I gave her time to digest the news that I had brought his medals. Neither one of us said a word. Agnes stared at me so suspiciously, I began to feel like a criminal. Although, if anyone ever did try to shoplift that junk of hers, she'd likely consider it an honor. We were both silent for so long, the buzzing of flies and the creaking of her fan began to sound as loud as a jackhammer. I reached inside my purse and pulled out the medals. I unwrapped them slowly and set them on the counter in front of her, being careful to turn each one face up out of respect.

"Clarence said they might get lost in the mail, so I—"

"Is that all Clarence said?"

"I don't know what you mean."

Agnes took a swallow of beer, rinsed it around in her

mouth like antiseptic, then asked, "How is Clarence? And Thelma, how is she doing?" I expected her to grab for the medals right away, but she didn't. It was almost as if she was preparing herself to touch them.

"She died last year," I said.

"I'm sorry to hear that." She set the beer bottle down quietly. "I only met Thelma a couple of times, when she visited with Clarence," said Agnes. "I liked her. I liked them both."

"They're good people."

"They are."

We stared at each other self-consciously until her hand finally reached over the counter. Her hands shook as she pulled the medals to herself and I heard her say "Johnny" under her breath. I expected a few tears, but didn't get them. It wasn't that she didn't love her son; I think she loved him too much to cry. She wouldn't allow herself the release. The pain was all she had left.

Her steely black eyes caught mine again. "You drove all this way to give me these, child?"

"No...no, I didn't. I made a detour down Route 66. I'm on my way to Austin." I wondered if maybe I shouldn't have mentioned the Mother Road, but once I had opened my big mouth, I couldn't ignore the topic. "I hope the Interstate doesn't take away your business," I said, knowing full well that it wouldn't only skim the top off her sales; it was going to stamp on her curio shop, spit on it, then laugh as it slowly withered and died.

"Too late for worry," she said. "Too late for that."

"What will you do?" I asked her.

"This is my home. I'm not leaving."

"Oh."

"At my age, it doesn't much matter," she said.

I didn't know how to respond, and was going to start telling Agnes about my meeting with Janis Joplin, but then I noticed a shelf on the wall behind her. Across it were photographs of Johnny—as a boy, at his high-school graduation, and in uniform. Nothing out of the ordinary until I scanned to the end of the row and saw one of him with Wendy Wood, obviously taken in Saskatoon since I recognized our garage in the background.

Why would Agnes put up a picture of Wendy Wood? She must have hundreds of photos of Johnny to choose from.

"Did Clarence take that photo of your son?"

She knew which one I meant right away and answered quickly. "Yes."

"That's Wendy Wood with him," I said. Then I added, "She never smiles. Maybe because she's missing teeth."

"Maybe."

I leaned over the counter to take a better look, and when I did, I could see that she was pregnant in the photograph. Pregnant with me.

I wondered if Agnes knew—if Clarence had told her that Wendy Wood was my real mother. Maybe Johnny had told her. Agnes had an odd look on her face, which made me suspect that she did know. Either way, Wendy wasn't worth mentioning. Janis was.

"I'm going to Kenneth Threadgill's bar to sing with Janis

Joplin," I said cheerily. "I met her in Saskatoon, and she's going to help me—"

"You sing?"

"I do. The blues. And some zydeco with my accordion. Music is my life."

"Like your mother."

"You mean Thelma?"

She paused. It was a long, dramatic kind of pause. The kind of pause where you can tell the other person is going to say something big. Or something they don't want to say.

"Wendy," she said.

"Wendy," I repeated.

"Johnny told me, Easy. About your mother."

"So he told you my nickname too."

"I like your name," she said.

Johnny and Agnes must have had nothing to talk about down here in the panhandle. Must have been one of those long, hot summer nights when you can't sleep, so they had nothing better to do than talk about Wendy Wood. And my nickname.

"She's not a bad person," said Agnes. "Not from what my son told me." She thought for a second. "You don't keep contact?"

"Never met her. Well, not since I was born. She's in a homeless shelter someplace in Calgary." Then for impact, I added, "I guess she's a prostitute." I heard myself say it and decided I was starting to sound like Marsha.

Agnes didn't like that remark; I could tell by the way she frowned and stitched her eyebrows together. What I couldn't figure out was why she was even the least bit interested in a nobody like Wendy. But for whatever reason, she kept it going.

"She loved to sing, same way you do. Was really good—that's what Johnny told me. But I guess her teeth ruined any chances for her to get ahead." She leaned back in her chair. "Meeting Janis Joplin wouldn't do her much good. Not without teeth." She shook her head. "That's too bad. Poor thing in a homeless shelter."

Poor thing? She didn't even bother to send me one letter. Not one Christmas card. Nothing.

I looked out the window and saw that Marsha was trying to find shade between the building and a spindly tree, so I figured it was time to get on my way. I was fed up with talking about Wendy Wood anyway. "Well, uh…it's been nice meeting you. My friend is waiting for me." As I spoke, my attention was diverted to an old car, parked behind the curio shop. It was a red convertible, and looked to be in decent shape, but it had been there for a long time because the grass had grown up in clumps around the tires.

Agnes lit another cigarette, stood up and peered out the window to see what I was looking at.

"Nice car," I said. "Is it yours?"

"Johnny's car. I don't drive."

"It's a great one. Looks like a Chevy convertible. What is it, a 1950—"

"1951 Chevy Styleline Deluxe," she replied.

I choked on her smoke, and she moved aside.

The car had a long deck, and a drop top. "You should have

it tuned up and learn to drive. A bit of body work here and there, and maybe some new upholstery, it'd be as good as new." I smiled at her. "And being a Chevy, no problem getting parts for it." I headed to the door. "Mind if I take a look?"

"Go ahead, child. But I can tell you, it doesn't need new upholstery."

I told Marsha I'd be another minute, then looked inside the window of the Chevy. Agnes wasn't kidding; the seats were like new. The odometer indicated that it had only been driven a short time—maybe a year or two—and from the condition of the paint, I could tell that Johnny had kept it away from anything corrosive. Still, being left out in the elements for the better part of twenty years meant that it did need work.

"Gonna be much longer?" asked Marsha, from where she sat with her back against the tree.

"No," I said, but my eyes never left the car. "You don't often find a twenty-year-old car that's barely been driven," I told her. "It's a gem."

Marsha didn't look at it, and didn't care about it, but managed to use it as a way of complaining about the yellow submarine. "Too bad you couldn't have found us a nicer car than the station wagon." The comment flew from her mouth like a little dart.

I ignored her and went back inside and told Agnes that the car was well worth getting refurbished, even if she just wanted to sell it.

"I'd never sell my son's car. Not even if my last penny was spent."

"He didn't drive it for very long."

"Two years. That's all. That's all the good Lord gave him." She looked up to the ceiling, like she was trying to see through it to heaven. "He drove it all the way to Saskatoon to take Clarence and Thelma for a ride—stayed there all summer that year."

"Bet he turned around for home when they started salting the roads," I said with a laugh, and Agnes offered up a little smile—only at the corners of her mouth, but it was there.

"Well, I think you should fix it up. It's a wonderful car." Marsha had made her way back into the yellow submarine, so I had to go. I didn't want to leave Agnes there, sitting all alone with nothing but the memory of her dead son and a whole bunch of Route 66 junk around her.

But Janis was waiting for me.

"On your way to Austin, is that right?" She followed me to the door.

"Yeah. Have to be there by tomorrow night, and it's a good eight-hour drive from here."

"Not traveling after dark, are you?" She looked out the window again. "Okay for that white friend of yours, but not for you."

"I'll be with her. I won't be alone. And we're going to spend tonight at a parish church that Marsha knows about—she's a postulant. It's somewhere around here."

Agnes let two streams of smoke come out her nose. "You're in Texas now," she said. "There's folks here that don't take kindly to people like us." I knew she meant black people. "Some folks are madder than ever these days. They're out for blood now." She sat back down. "Be careful, child."

CHAPTER FIFTEEN

Marsha took a turn at the wheel, since she was the one who'd been given the directions to St. Michael's Parish. Of course, she managed to get them fouled up, and we ended up in the middle of nowhere. I'd told her to write everything down, but she insisted she could remember. And Marsha making a decision was like carving Mount Rushmore; once it was done it was done, and you didn't dare suggest any changes. We were so far off the beaten path, I couldn't even find a mailbox to mail my postcard. After having it in my hand for two hours, the ink was starting to smear, so I jammed it back inside my purse.

Our plan was to stay overnight at the parish church (the one that was supposed to be near Amarillo), then make our way to Fort Worth the next day. From there, we'd take the I-35 to Austin (although after seeing what was happening to businesses along Route 66, I had become an official hater of all Interstates). But somehow we missed our turn, and soon the long shadows of evening started draping themselves across rooftops and fields. When the first star blinked in the sky, I knew we had about as much hope of finding the parish as Roy did Yasgur's Farm.

I was starving by that time. Marsha should have been, having had no lunch, but those nuts and seeds sustained her the way they would a hibernating ground squirrel.

"That sign said fifty miles to Wichita Falls," I told her, unfolding a highway map across my lap. I turned on the interior light, and decided that our plans needed to change. "We'll have to find somewhere to sleep. I can't waste any more time trying to locate St. Michael's. Tomorrow we can hit the I-35 which will take us right into Austin."

Marsha wanted to try a bit longer, so on we drove, figuring that at the very least we'd find a place to eat. On the way from Saskatoon to Albuquerque, I had enjoyed night driving—the cheerful glimpses of families watching television, a baby in its father's arms, children silhouetted in a window. But this stretch of highway in Texas felt different. It didn't have the warmth of Highway 85, nor the nostalgia of Route 66. It resonated something dark and sinister.

When we finally stumbled upon a diner, it had no neon sign, just sputtery little bulbs, most of which were burned out, and trees that were bare except at the very top, like someone had chopped off every branch they could reach. Inside, a long counter was lined with round seats, and tables were scattered haphazardly around the room.

Everyone's eyes stood out on stalks when Marsha and I entered the place. I presumed it was her nun outfit that was the problem, although I soon realized that the gapes were aimed in my direction.

When a guy came out from behind the counter—he was the cook and the waiter and likely the owner too—and headed straight for me, it confirmed that I was the problem, not Marsha.

The restaurant fell silent—the kind of all-embracing silence that can make the dropping of a fork sound like a pistol shot.

"You're not welcome here. Git out." He pointed to the door.

A woman with sagging purple cheeks turned in her chair to get a good look at me, and smiled and nodded at the owner as if to say "Good for you, Charlie. Give that black girl what she has coming to her."

I'm not sure from whence it came—maybe from watching Sidney Poitier in *In the Heat of the Night*—but somehow I found a reserve of strength that enabled me to fight back.

Be careful, said Thelma. *Walk, but don't run.*

"My friend and I have been driving a long way, and we're hungry. Can I please have—"

"Git your black ass out of here," he said. Now everyone in the diner was watching, and every single one of them was pleased with what was happening.

"You do know that it's against the law to discriminate," I said. I could taste the salty perspiration on my upper lip.

He laughed. "The law? You want the law?" The woman with the purple cheeks laughed too, then said something to the man beside her.

"I'll call my cousin. He's the sheriff. I'm sure he'll be happy to drive you out to the county limits." He laughed. "He's got a rifle in his trunk."

"Let's go," said Marsha. She was pale with fright.

"I'm from Canada," I said frantically, as if that would make a difference.

"Negro-loving Canada. Home of the free," said the cook/waiter/owner. He opened the door and stood there with his foot in it. "Go back to Canada. They can keep you. But git your goddamn black ass out of my diner, or I'll string you up to that tree out back. Do you hear me?"

Marsha prodded me out the door. Through the front window of the diner, I could see all the smiling and leering and laughing faces, and I felt completely humiliated. Degraded. Ashamed, even. Of what, I don't know, but I was ashamed.

Ten thousand Miss Poultices, twenty thousand George Penns—nothing could ever add up to what it felt like to be thrown out of that restaurant.

Marsha put an arm around me and I saw tears in her big, scared eyes. Then she hugged me, and I wanted to cry. I didn't—I couldn't, because it would have meant that horrible man had won. But I wanted to. I wanted to yell out loud or throw a brick through the window or get a skywriter to spell *B-i-g-o-t* over his stupid diner. But trying to grab hold of my emotions was like trying to catch minnows with my fingers;

everything slipped away from me, and all I could do was let Marsha hug me. I think it probably did her more good than me, since by the way she hugged me—with flat hands against my shoulders—I could tell she wasn't used to hugging. Maybe she'd never been hugged in her life. And because she was so sharp-cornered, a hug from Marsha felt like being squeezed between a pair of two-by-fours.

I was sick and asked Marsha to drive, and we drove and drove and drove and drove. She said nothing; I said nothing. When we came upon another restaurant, Marsha went inside and brought out milkshakes and fries for us, while I waited in the car, covering my face when anyone walked by. This time I was the one who could only manage a few bites; my appetite had disappeared, and I felt as if I would vomit even the smallest mouthful of food.

Because it was after midnight by that time, and we had long since given up hope of locating the parish, I convinced Marsha that we had to sleep in the car. There was no way I was going to try to check into a motel—not without Sidney Poitier, the Negro Motorist Green book, and a bulletproof vest.

After an hour of feeling sorry for myself, and going over everything Thelma had told me about how she and Clarence had dealt with the most abysmal situations, I emerged from the darkest part of my tunnel of misery. Still, I wanted a distraction, so I struck up a conversation with Marsha. I didn't care what she had to say, I was ready to listen.

"So have you decided on a name?" I asked her. "Is it going to be Bohuslava? God's glory?"

CAROLINE STELLINGS

"Yes, Louisiana, I think that Bohuslava is the name I will take." She said it with the kind of mystic reverence normally reserved for an eclipse of the sun, but there was ketchup on her face, which detracted from the whole "God's glory" thing.

"How come you never call me Easy?" I asked her, figuring it was because she didn't believe in anything that wasn't difficult.

"I prefer to call you Louisiana," she said, sounding more like a schoolteacher than a traveling companion.

She opened up the car door to look at the sky. It was brilliant with sparkling stars, and Marsha seemed lost in thought. When the air began to cool down, she closed it again and stretched out along the front seat. I moved to the middle. I couldn't sleep for the longest time, but felt drowsy, and started up another chat—the kind that you can only have when you're half asleep.

"Why did you decide to become a nun?" I bravely asked.

Marsha didn't answer at first, then finally replied, "I had a calling."

"You mean like Jesus appeared in your room one night?"

"Something like that."

I didn't believe her. I knew that she'd chosen to do it so she could be better than everyone else.

"What did your parents say?"

"They don't know yet."

"Don't know yet? But—" I had to think for a minute to do some calculations. "You've been a postulant for months now. You're taking your name in October, so you've been a postulant for…"

"Three months."

"So you haven't seen your parents since April?" I asked.

"February."

"February? Don't you like your parents?"

"It has nothing to do with like or dislike," she said. "They are traveling in Europe."

I tried to find out if she ever wrote to them, or if they ever called her, but Marsha snipped off between her teeth any loose threads of our conversation. I got the picture that she had been raised in a cold family and could see why she didn't know how to hug. When I first met Marsha, I figured that something in her childhood had turned her sour—maybe some kid had called her "toothpick legs" or peeled all the wrappings off her crayons. After a while though, I realized that her problems stemmed from something deep-seated. I didn't feel sorry for her exactly, but I didn't detest her quite as much, once I knew she'd been starved of affection.

Marsha finally drifted off to sleep, her faint snoring sounding like a fly buzzing behind a curtain. I guess I fell asleep too, because before I knew it, the sun was beginning to stretch and yawn, the air inside the car was hot, and Friday, the tenth of July, had finally arrived. I awoke with a tight, expectant feeling, and with the coming of morning, life didn't seem nearly as bad as it had the night before. The anticipation of singing with Janis overrode the idiots at the diner by a Texas mile.

I threw myself into the driver's seat and managed to find the Interstate fairly quickly. After a week of travel, it dawned on me that I was about to meet my destiny, and it felt like the wheels of the station wagon never hit the highway. I was so excited to think that Threadgill's and Janis were at the end of the road that nothing else mattered. Even Marsha seemed different to me. Although she didn't jump for joy, she didn't complain about my singing the way she usually did; I guess she knew I had to practice. I did Bessie Smith and Billie Holiday songs mostly, but I threw in some Janis too.

It was right after I sang "Piece of My Heart" that Marsha reminded me that she would not be going to Threadgill's, not even for a minute, and would be going straight to the convent in Austin. She planned on spending the day there before returning to Albuquerque on Saturday. She made it clear that she'd rather take a picnic lunch to the morgue than go with me to the bar.

"But Mother Grace said your assignment was to meet Janis," I protested. "You aren't going to lie to her, are you?"

"I feel too ill to go."

"No, you don't."

"Yes, I do."

"You're not sick."

"Am too."

Big baby, I thought. "Well, I won't say anything. I'm not a rat. But you're missing out on the experience of a lifetime. I mean, c'mon, this is Janis Joplin we're talking about. *Pearl!*"

"Pearl?"

"That's what she calls herself, when she wears the feather boas and wild clothes," I explained. "That's what she told me to call her!"

"What a vain and self-centered thing to do. She should be happy with the name her parents gave her," she said, her lips folded in like a buttonhole.

"You're changing your name, aren't you?"

"That's different. A nun takes a new name to show that she has given up her life to serve God."

"No, it isn't different at all. Janis has given up her life in order to serve the public. As a performer."

"Rubbish," said Marsha. "That name Pearl—well, it sounds like something a whore would use."

"You're wrong," I said. "I remember Thelma telling me that pearls are the result of sand getting into the shell of an oyster. The irritation is what makes the silky fluid flow."

"So?"

"She said it's like trouble in your life. Without it, you don't amount to much. Without something abrasive, you never find out what you're made of. I think that's why Janis chose that name. Because life's been tough on her, but she realizes that without her problems, she'd never have become such a great singer."

Marsha didn't reply for a long time—several miles at least.

"Anyway," I continued, "I think Pearl is a wonderful name."

"I think it sounds cheap. Is it her intention to sound common?"

"I don't know," I admitted, looking at my watch. "But we're nearly there, so why don't you change your mind, come to Threadgill's, and ask her yourself?" I wrinkled up my forehead and scowled. "What are you afraid of?"

"Nothing. I don't want to go there, that's all."

"I thought nuns were supposed to go places they didn't want to. Learn about life in the gutter."

Marsha sneered, then I sneered, but since we were getting close to Austin, I pulled over so that she and I could change places. I wanted to read the map carefully so we didn't miss our exit, and I didn't trust Marsha to do it right.

Once we were back on the road, and I was sure we were on track, I decided to bug her again. "Didn't Mother Grace say the Grey Nuns were brave women who risked their lives to help people sick with typhus and cholera?" I hadn't listened to everything she'd told us about the history of the order, but I remembered that part.

Marsha didn't say a word. But she knew I was right.

I don't know why I argued with her. I didn't want her to come to Threadgill's, and I didn't care about her career as a nun. Maybe I was too nervous to go there alone, and Marsha was better than nothing.

Maybe it was worse than that.

Maybe I was afraid of what I had to face once I got inside.

CHAPTER SIXTEEN

Marsha pulled into Threadgill's and waited while I took my suitcase, accordion, and frottoir out of the back of the yellow submarine. It was one of those toe-tapping waits that said she wanted the hell out of there. At least my lecture about the Grey Nuns had put a temporary stop on those knife-edged statements of hers. She still looked like she was smelling something putrid, though, every time Janis was mentioned.

"I'll be staying at the convent tonight," she told me. She had rolled the window down an inch, and was talking to me through the crack. "Will you be returning to Albuquerque with me tomorrow?"

"No," I said. "I'm hoping Mr. Threadgill asks me to stay. Or better yet, maybe Janis—I mean, Pearl—will ask me to come to California with her."

Marsha rolled up the window.

"Wait!" I hollered.

"What is it?" This time she opened the window only half an inch.

"Well…uh…good-bye. I hope things—you…" Trying to say good-bye to Marsha was impossible, partly because I was talking to my own reflection in the window, and partly because she was so anxious to get away that she kept letting up on the brake and jerking the car ahead.

"Yes. Thank you. Take care."

She sounded more like a pharmacist than a friend. Okay, maybe we weren't pals exactly, but *take care?* She drove off in that same choky cloud of dust as she had on the first day I met her, being sure not to let any part of her gaze fall on Threadgill's. I waved. She didn't. And that was that.

♪

Electrified with hope, but feeling like I'd just boarded an ocean liner with no ticket and no passport, I made my way to the front door. The place was brimming with people, too many to count, and when I asked a guy, he told me that the gathering was to celebrate Ken Threadgill's birthday. He also said that Janis wasn't there yet.

Tobacco smoke had discolored the whitewashed walls of the converted gas station, and bluegrass music reverberated from every one of them. I squeezed my way in and wondered how, in all the chaos, I was ever going to get Janis's attention.

A waitress saw my instruments and assumed I was with one of the bands; she had eyebrows that were two hairs wide

with azure-blue shadow underneath each one. She pulled me
through the crowd to where the musicians had put their stuff,
and showed me a safe place to leave my suitcase, not far from
the stage. She handed me a beer and didn't ask for I.D.

When I saw an older guy in a cowboy hat I guessed that he
was Threadgill, since he was clearly the center of attention. He
wasn't dressed up, and seemed like a laid-back kind of guy. Not
pretentious at all. The band played a country tune, then pushed
him to a microphone. He sang "T for Texas," an old favorite
that wasn't exactly a favorite of mine, but everyone around me
loved it. I hoped that when Janis came, she'd sing some blues,
then I could do the same.

*Maybe she's forgotten all about the Southern Comfort and
all about me.*

Maybe she's not coming.

Maybe she decided to go directly to Los Angeles.

I set my instruments on a chair and found another for
myself. A middle-aged man with Brylcreem in his parted-down-
the-middle hair plunked himself next to me. He smelled like
stale wine with a dash of garlic and a hint of tooth decay, and
I wondered why it's always the ones with the worst breath that
are the most anxious to corner you.

"You know, a few years ago, you couldn't have been here,"
he said, like he was telling me something I didn't know. Like I
wasn't aware that the place was once a segregated venue.

I didn't reply.

I looked around though, and realized that everyone was
white.

Why didn't I notice that right away? This is Austin, for God's sake. Why did Janis ask me to come here? Threadgill doesn't want me to play in his bar. He's only doing it as a favor for Janis.

Maybe she'll take me with her to California.

Confusing thoughts swirled around in my head, and my self-confidence was dragging somewhere around my ankles.

"A few years ago, you couldn't have—" His breath was so strong, you could get high on a few whiffs.

"I was asked to come here."

"Okay." He put his arm around me and I stood up.

"You look tired," he said. "Let's get out of here and go to my place." He rose from his chair and tried to shove me against a wall. I was trying to decide whether to kick him in the groin or yell "Fire!" when the waitress who'd given me the beer grabbed him by the back of his collar and turned him over to a bouncer.

"Thanks. A lot," I said.

"Don't mention it," she told me.

Before she got away, I confided in her. "Will there be trouble with me being here?" Then I added, "I'm from Canada, and well, I'm not familiar—"

"We follow the law, honey," she said. And while it was comforting to hear that I wasn't going to be thrown out by the scruff of my neck the way Mr. Brylcreem had been, knowing that I was being tolerated because Threadgill had no choice made me feel about as welcome as a skunk at a garden party.

"Threadgill's a racist?"

"No, not really. He's just trying to run a business. Doesn't want any trouble." She shrugged. "Keep to yourself and there'll be no problems."

Keep to myself? Don't mingle with dem white folks?

The waitress picked up her tray and vanished into the crowd.

Just as I began to wonder why Janis had asked me there in the first place, every head swiveled around in the direction of the side door. I knew it had to be her without even looking. Sure enough, people starting yelling out her name and whistling.

She strolled confidently to the stage area, not far from where I stood. I took a good look at her; she was as vivacious as ever, but her eyes were redder than before, half-closed and murky.

She was high on heroin.

She grabbed Threadgill, threw a necklace of flowers around his neck, then hollered out in an exaggerated Texas drawl, "I brought you the one thing I knew you'd like, Ken—a good lei." One thing about Janis, she didn't hold back.

It turned out she'd just been to Honolulu, because the next thing she said was, "I can't play rock'n'roll without mah band, and mah band is in Hawaii."

Good, I thought. *Then she can sing some blues songs instead.*

After she and Threadgill gave each other far too many hugs and how-have-you-beens, everyone screamed for her to take the stage. She stumbled up the step, then asked for a guitar. She had arrived with an entourage of people—who they were, I had no idea—but one of them appeared to be a manager or agent or something, because he clenched his teeth like a movie director then handed her a six-string.

"I can't tune it. I can't tune worth shit," she complained. "Somebody tune this thing."

Somebody did, and she sang two Kris Kristofferson songs. Because country music ranked with elevator music in my mind, I was disappointed at first. "Sunday Mornin' Comin' Down" was okay, and everyone laughed when she joked, "almost as bad as Tuesday morning coming down, or Thursday morning coming down." Judging by the way she was sucking on her Southern Comfort (not the bottle I'd given her—she'd probably gone through a dozen since then) and by the fresh needle tracks on her arms I glimpsed when she pulled up her sleeve to hold the guitar, I'd say she'd had a lot of experience in coming down.

But none of that—not the alcohol, nor the heroin, nor the fact that she was singing country tunes—detracted from hearing her sing "Me and Bobby McGee" live and from only a few feet away. Her voice penetrated my body and soul like nothing ever had before. Like nothing ever would again.

Busted flat in Baton Rouge

From the first few lines I knew I was witnessing something spectacular. Janis Joplin wasn't a well-trained singer; she wasn't even a particularly good guitar player. Her vibrant alto voice was earthy and twangy, and I loved it, but even that didn't explain why everyone in the room was mesmerized by her. Janis had something inexplicable—something I knew I'd never have.

Freedom's just another word
for nothing left to lose...

That was it. Right there. That was the clue.

Janis was one hundred percent free. Free of inhibitions. Free of fear. And, some might say, free of the self-control that would have stopped her from addiction. But Janis didn't allow any shackles on her life. That's why, when she sang, she took everyone to that same place of freedom. And that's why, when she sang, it felt so good.

She finished the song to a room full of ecstatic screaming. I looked into her eyes, and oddly, despite all the attention and love from the audience, they were dead.

It wasn't my place to analyze her, but it didn't take a genius to see that despite bringing life to everyone around her, she had killed a part of herself in the process. *Like Jesus*, I told myself. And given the scars on her arms, I wasn't far off the mark.

I wasn't sure if I should remind her that she invited me to sing, or if I should wait until she noticed me. I didn't know if she'd even recognize me.

She chatted with people she knew, and after about ten minutes, her eyes caught mine. She pointed at me with her cigarette, then smiled. That was when I knew that all the anticipatory days leading up to that moment had been worth it.

"What's your name again? Wait! Louisiana. That's right. I really dig that name." She grabbed one of her friends, an attractive woman whom I could tell was a Californian from the clothes she wore, and explained our chance meeting in Saskatoon.

"She's terrific," Janis told her. "She plays zydeco on her accordion and frottoir—did you bring them?" She looked at the chair next to me. "You did! Yeah!"

Speechless, and trying to think of something just this side of human sacrifice to show my appreciation, I must have appeared foolish, but the whole scene—one that I had acted out in my head seven hundred times by then—transported me to some kind of a dream world.

Janis pulled the Southern Comfort out of her purse and took a swig. She offered it to me, but I declined.

"Every fucking bottle but this," she told her friend. "And Leezy...Louisie—"

"Easy."

"Oh, God, I love that name." When she leaned toward me, her breath was sweet and warm. "Are you ready to sing?"

And then, exactly then, at the moment I'd been waiting for my whole life, with *Janis Joplin* asking *me*, Louisiana Merritt, to sing the blues at the very place where she had been discovered, Thelma came into my head. And this time, nothing would get her to leave. She wouldn't even wait her turn.

Think of all the black folks, Easy. Think of them.

Think of all the black singers that would have given their right arm to sing at Threadgill's but weren't allowed in the door.

Bessie Smith wouldn't have been allowed to sing there. Billie Holiday would have been tossed out with the garbage. Janis, now she glorifies these women right down to their faults, their addictions. You can go that route, Easy. Or you can honor them another way—by standing for something.

What are you going to do, Easy?

I picked up my accordion and frottoir, and headed for the stage, determined that nothing would stop me from singing, not even Thelma.

Janis cheered me on.

I sat my instruments down on the stage and looked out to the audience. I watched as Janis whispered something to Threadgill—maybe she was apologizing for my being black.

Apologizing. Because I was black.

If I'd been white, she wouldn't have needed to.

Looking back at that moment, I don't know if I made the right choice or not. I'll never know. But I thought about Clarence and Thelma, and Agnes and Johnny. I thought about Bessie Smith and Billie Holiday. I thought about myself.

And I decided not to sing.

Even though it meant the end of my career as a blues singer.

I picked up my things, and walked over to Janis. The crowd made sounds—a mixture of boos and whispers and questions—and Threadgill took over the stage to calm everybody down.

"I'm sorry," I told her, "but the only reason I'm allowed to sing here is because of you. If I'd been any other black singer, they would have told me to hit the road."

Janis didn't say anything. She made no comment at all. Deep in thought, she dragged on her cigarette with more force than usual.

I headed through the building, past the gawking crowd

once again. I didn't feel threatened, the way I did in the diner. But I was certain that a lot of things were being said about me— things that weren't true. I wanted to shout out and explain, but that would have only made things worse. The only thing left to do was keep walking, and never look back.

It seemed like an hour before I finally found my way to the front entrance.

When I did, Marsha was standing inside the door.

CHAPTER SEVENTEEN

Judging by the look on her face, it was clear that Marsha had entered Threadgill's with the same amount of enthusiasm as Daniel must have had when entering the lion's den.

"I came," she said, sounding like a coiled spring of willpower.

"Good for you."

Marsha's two steps into the bar were the farthest thing from my mind, so if she was looking for congratulations from me, she wasn't going to get them.

"I did it," she said, in the same tone of voice as someone who'd finally gone through with a root canal.

"Good for you," I repeated. "Now I'm leaving." I squeezed past her and started for the road. I figured on hitchhiking to the airport then heading for home. Back to the garage. Back to being a grease monkey. At least I could look myself in the mirror.

Marsha shadowed behind me, and it was like being in kindergarten again and having the kid with jam on his face follow you everywhere you went.

"Oh, what is it?" I snapped.

"What happened? Didn't you sing?"

"What do you care if I sang or not? You hate music except for hymns, you can't stand me, and you've always treated my desire to sing as a recurring illness. Like malaria."

"That is incorrect," she said, sounding like a schoolteacher again.

I turned to leave, and would have made it to the road, except that Janis found me, and Janis is one of those people you don't walk away from.

She pushed her round Foster Grants to the top of her head, then screamed at me. "Hey!" A bunch of people had trailed her out the door and were clambering around, so she motioned to a couple of bouncers. "Get them out of my hair," she insisted. "G'wan!" She shooed them away. Once they'd dispersed, she found a place to sit on a picnic bench, plunked down her liquor bottle, lit another cigarette, and hollered at me again.

"Get the hell over here!"

I walked back, feeling uneasy about what I'd done. Marsha came too, but her attitude was completely different—she resembled a high-ranking officer being forced to intermingle with the recruits.

"Sit down," said Janis, and I did.

Marsha stood.

There was a moment of silence while Janis let smoke out of her mouth and it hovered around her like a genie. Then I spoke up.

"I'm sorry," was all I could muster. I was going to say something about my conscience—how it stopped me from singing. But Janis knew that already, and it would have sounded pretentious. After all, it had been six years since Dylan wrote that *the times, they were a-changin'*. Who was I to argue? And I knew that Janis had always gone out of her way to venerate the black singers like Bessie Smith who had influenced her.

"Ken's not a racist," said Janis, as if she was reading my mind. "He's just tryin' to run a business, is all. I mean he started serving beer here in the forties, for God's sake. He's a good ol' boy, you know?"

I didn't argue with Janis Joplin.

Marsha did.

"He could be arrested. It's against the law to segregate," she said, and while it was nice of her to stand up for me, it wasn't very helpful. It was like being held up by a gunman and having a little old lady slam him with her purse.

"Mr. Threadgill didn't stop me from singing," I told Marsha.

"The place is filled with assholes," said Janis. "I don't blame you for walking away." She and Marsha stared at each other for a Texas minute. Janis was trying to figure out if Marsha was a Mennonite or just a square, and Marsha was aghast at the fact that Janis was braless.

"Are you a—"

Marsha interrupted her. "I'm a postulant." When she said the word *postulant*, she rose a foot off the ground.

"Gonna be a nun?" Janis took a swig of her booze. Marsha indicated her disapproval by turning her lips into a small pink rosette, but she answered the question.

"Yes."

I waited for her to say, *so what you gonna do about it?* She didn't.

Then Janis surprised us all.

"Good for you," she remarked, and I was pretty sure she knew what she was saying, although she still looked glassy-eyed and disheveled, like somebody'd put her head in a blender. Then she had questions for Marsha. "When do you take your vows or whatever it is you do?"

"The first week in October I will become a novice and take my new name. Then I'll be serving the church in Calgary. My vows come later." She said it with such finality, I felt like putting a Rest In Peace wreath around her neck.

"I was just in Calgary," said Janis. "Before Hawaii. Hell of a show. Can't remember any of it."

They stared at each other again, so I decided to explain why Marsha was with me.

"She and another nun, Sister Beatrice, were on their way to Albuquerque—they're staying there for the summer to learn about the mission—so I got a ride with them. To save money."

"Albuquerque," repeated Janis, taking another swig. "So what are you doing in Austin?"

I wondered if Marsha was going to tell her the truth, hedge

the question, or just plain lie. When she took on that sepulchral tone again, I knew she'd decided to go with the first option.

"I was ordered by the Mother Superior to meet you."

Janis laughed so loud that Marsha shook her head to get her hearing back.

"Me? What the hell for? To show you what not to do?"

"No." Marsha swelled her nostrils. "To learn about—well, to experience—"

"G'wan," said Janis, blowing smoke into the air. "Give it to me straight."

I cringed, hoping she wouldn't, but she did.

"Mother Superior wants me to understand the nature of heroin addiction so that I will be ready for my work with drug-dependent teens."

When Janis left that sentence hanging there, I decided I'd better try to soften it a bit.

"That's not it—not exactly," I declared. "You see there's this young man in Albuquerque who the Mother Superior is trying to help. His name is Roy and she thinks he's going to die from heroin. She's really worried about him, and thought that meeting you would be the best thing for him."

Janis raised her eyebrows, so I continued.

"He grabs people's arms to see if they can pull him back in."

While that remark wouldn't make sense to anyone else, Janis nodded, as if she knew exactly what Roy was trying to do.

"He told us that *you* could pull him back in—if he could grab your arm—because you know what it's like to wrestle with…well, addiction. I guess." I took a deep breath and kept trying to explain. "He thought I was on my way to Yasgur's and begged me to take him along."

"So where is he?" asked Janis.

"Well, uh—" Marsha cut in. "He's still in Albuquerque. He couldn't make it."

Boy, for a nun, she's an excellent liar. Did it with a straight face even.

Janis started removing bangles one by one from her forearm. At first, I thought she was going to show us her track marks, but then I realized she was trying to get at one of the bracelets. Many of them were cheap plastic things, or beads, but halfway up her arm was a real nice one. It looked like it was solid gold. She pulled it off and handed it to Marsha.

"Give this to Roy."

When Janis handed her the bangle, Marsha looked at it disdainfully, holding it between two fingers as if she was dispensing of it like a dirty tissue. She dropped it into the side pocket of her purse.

Somebody called out to Janis, and she told them she'd be there in a minute, so I knew my time with her was about to end. I wondered what she was going to say to me. As it turned out, she was more interested in Marsha.

"First week in October, eh?"

"Yes, Miss Joplin."

What do you know? Marsha's finally showing some respect for the world-famous singer. Or is she just trying to keep her distance?

"Oh, for Christ's sake—oops! Not *Miss Joplin*." Janis cackled again. "Call me Pearl."

I smiled, Marsha looked at the ground, and Janis got up to leave.

"So what's your new name gonna be?" she asked Marsha.

Marsha didn't reply, so I did.

"She can't decide between Sister Bohuslava or Sister Ivanna. And another one I can't remember."

"Sister Nastasiya," said Marsha.

"Do they mean something?" asked Janis, and when Marsha explained all those holier-than-thou names, the singer looked puzzled, then said, "I'm no nun, that's for sure, but maybe your name should be something easier to say. You know, for guys like Roy."

I agreed with Janis.

"Easy?" Janis put her hand on my shoulder.

"Yeah?"

"Can you get to California?"

"To sing?"

Of course to sing, you idiot. She isn't inviting you to clean her house.

"When I'm done touring, I'm heading to Los Angeles to record an album. I'll be done by the end of September, or early in October. Then I'll have some time. There's some people—I'd like them to hear you, 'cause I think you're great." She staggered again, then picked up her bag. "Are you going back to Saskatoon—I could take down your number and call you there."

I quickly grabbed a pen from my purse and scrambled to find a piece of paper. All I had was an old invoice from the garage, but it did the trick. I wrote down all the information, neatly and clearly, then handed it back to her. She shoved it into her bag, not nearly as carefully as I'd wished. But at least it was in there. Right then, Janis was ambushed by a bunch of fans demanding autographs and grabbing onto her like she was the last available antidote for a worldwide epidemic of some killer disease.

They loved her, they loved her music, they loved the new Bobby McGee song. Love, love, love. By the time they'd confessed all this love, and Janis had given them everything she could (then had a bouncer get rid of them), it was as if she'd been to the blood-donor clinic about seventeen times, all in the same day. She was drained.

No sooner did that group dissolve than another formed, and I wondered if she'd survive it.

The second wave was meaner than the first. They were in love with Janis, just as the first group had been, but a few of them made it clear with gestures and facial expressions that they didn't like me. No one said anything—probably because it was a well-known fact that Janis did not tolerate racism—but they made me feel uncomfortable nonetheless.

While running into people like that was inevitable, and after what happened to me in Denver and Wichita Falls, I almost expected to be put down, what I didn't anticipate was their turning their attention to Marsha.

"What the hell's that thing on your head?" said one of the young women, a tough-looking chick with black globules at the end of her eyelashes.

Marsha shook from the top of her head to the bottom of her skinny legs. If one of them had so much as brushed against her, I think she would have shattered into a million pieces.

"I said, what is that thing?" demanded the tough one.

"Leave her alone," I said.

Then Janis cut in. "What's your fucking problem? You got a problem with nuns?"

The bunch of them started to laugh.

"Nun!" The tough one leered contemptuously at poor Marsha, who must have felt like she'd just peed her pants. (It's a wonder she didn't, but she seldom drinks liquids.)

I felt sorry for her, and realized why she preferred to hang out in convents and churches; at the same time, I could see why Mother Grace had insisted she face the real world and learn to live in it.

Janis gave them all a piece of her mind.

"You're bastards," she told them. She called them a lot of other things, too, most of which I don't think Marsha had ever heard before.

The young woman with the mascara mumbled something, but by then her friends were busy trying to get Janis's autograph. A bouncer got rid of them eventually, then Janis said to Marsha, "Good luck, honey. It ain't gonna be an easy life. I admire you." She pulled down her sunglasses over her eyes, stuck her bottle back into her bag (I hoped she'd put the lid on tight, because she threw it right on top of my address), and headed back to the bar. Then she turned and said to Marsha, "Tell Roy something for me, will ya? Tell him to live in the moment, man. Tell him—tell him that in the end, it's all the same fucking day."

And while it was clear that Marsha was horrorstruck by Janis's language, and appalled by her alcoholism and drug abuse, I could tell that she was completely taken off guard when Janis said that she admired her. Partly because she hadn't expected the singer to be the least bit interested in religion, but mostly because Marsha didn't think anyone admired her.

CHAPTER EIGHTEEN

I could tell by the way Janis shoved my address into her bag carelessly and without folding it first that she would never call me at the end of September. And why should she? I'd had my chance, and I'd blown it. She offered me the opportunity of a lifetime, an opportunity that would never show itself again, and instead of running with it, I allowed the idealist in me to ruin everything. And why was I being so self-righteous? You'd think I was Martin Luther King Jr., the way I acted. I only had my big stupid self to blame for losing out.

And Thelma. I blamed her, too. I blamed her for bringing my dream down to its knees.

And now I was heading back to Saskatoon with nothing more than my pride and a bottomless cup of regrets.

Even though Marsha and I had planned on taking a more direct route back to the Sisters of Charity convent, since we weren't going through Amarillo this time, it was still going to be a ten-hour drive. So after we'd left Threadgill's, we drove first to Notre Dame, a Catholic school outside the city, to spend the night in the nun's residence. I'd decided that hitchhiking to the airport was a dumb idea; it wasn't that I minded dying so much, I just didn't want to be murdered. So I chose to ride with Marsha the following day to Albuquerque, say good-bye to Mother Grace, and from there, take a flight home.

Notre Dame was not a cheery bless-this-house kind of place, it was as cold as a crypt—not an easy thing to accomplish in the heart of Texas, where the sun baked the moisture out of even the shadiest place. The walls were cement, the furniture was old, and the lodgings felt more like the Bastille than a place for nuns to live. I thought about how in the novel *Dracula*, Jonathan Harker took refuge with nuns after jumping out the window of the vampire's castle. If he had wound up at this place, he'd have wondered if he'd made the right choice.

Except for the prayers before and after eating, there was little conversation at dinner; everyone just sat there, chewing, swallowing, and watching each other grow. They led such dull lives that ordinarily, I would have felt like it was my duty to liven things up, but I was too depressed myself. I was seated next to a woman with a tiny head like a shriveled coconut, and a nasal voice. When she finally asked if I was joining the organization—I assumed she meant the sisterhood and not the mob—I shrugged and took another bite of watery creamed corn. If she'd asked me a few hours earlier, I would have thrown back my shoulders and declared that I was going to be a blues singer. Now, I figured the sisterhood might not be a bad idea. Or the mob.

However bleak the events of that day had been, and however dreadful they made me feel, they had the exact opposite effect on Marsha. Normally one of those rare individuals who could stop after eating one potato chip, she was consuming her food (even the creamed corn) with more gusto than I'd seen from her. And even though she'd never admit to finding Janis more tolerable than she'd anticipated, and even though she'd never own up to the fact that meeting the singer was the most exciting thing that had ever happened in her monotonous life, I noticed that her usual pallor had turned to an almost healthy shade of pink. Ever since Janis had said that she admired her, Marsha had held her head higher and extended her arms farther; she even looked a tad fatter. It was like someone had stuffed a rag doll.

After dinner, I was assigned a dismal little room at the end of an unlit corridor. About an hour after we'd all turned in for the night, and I ventured out into the hall to get my accordion and frottoir, the nun with the shriveled head materialized out of the darkness to tell me it wasn't allowed. I insisted on taking my purse, though, and set it on the bed beside me. That was when I found the postcard I'd written in Tucumcari.

The postcard got me thinking about Clarence, and, in turn, about Thelma.

I wished she had just stayed out of my head until after my performance. That's the trouble with good people. They make you feel that you have to be good too, and if you're not, the guilt pounds away at your brain and makes whatever bad thing you decide to do not worth it in the end.

Just because Austin was home to a lot of racists, it didn't mean the entire state was. Couldn't Thelma have let it go, just this once? For me?

God knows, she forgave Clarence the worst sin of all and without a single repercussion. She never used the affair with Wendy Wood against him. Not even once.

On the wall, over a dusty chest-of-drawers, I spotted a framed print. It said *Judge not, Lest Ye be Judged* and had small blue flowers and green vines around it.

That one should be hanging in Marsha's room, not mine, I told myself. *She judges everyone she meets. Everyone.*

Thelma never did. Just look at how she forgave my father.

Why did she forgive Clarence?

All of this played through my mind as I tried to get to sleep on an old hard bed with a metal crucifix hanging on the wall, two inches from the back of my head, like I was dead. I might as well have been—lying there in that gloomy room I decided that happiness was nothing but an illusion. I closed my eyes, but couldn't sleep.

Something was bothering me. Brewing inside me. With all the excitement of meeting Janis, and the horrible disappointment that followed, it wasn't until I was alone in that dreary residence that I had the time to think things through.

Why did Agnes act so weird when I arrived at her store?

Why did she keep that picture of Wendy Wood?

Despite my best efforts to put the pieces together I couldn't, and exhaustion set in. Before I knew it, I was back in the yellow submarine with Marsha, sailing at a good clip down the highway. What had started out as an exciting excursion to Austin, turned into a miserable return trip to the Sisters of Charity convent. I didn't feel like talking about anything—nothing—and Marsha was deep in thought, a place in which I was happy to leave her. She champed on her seeds while she ruminated over something, grinding up conceptions inside her head to the rhythm of the molars in her cheeks. I think she was trying to figure out why such a wicked and sinful woman like Janis admired her, and whether it was wicked and sinful to appreciate being admired by a wicked and sinful woman.

Because we'd left Notre Dame so early in the morning, we made good time on the road. And since neither one of us had much to say, and didn't bother with sightseeing or even taking time to eat (she had her seeds, and I had no appetite), we made it back to Albuquerque by five o'clock that afternoon.

Mother Grace and Sister Beatrice were making supper when we arrived, and were serving up what appeared to be chili. I reached for a cold drink, but quickly threw it back into the cooler when Mother Grace spotted us. She made no attempt to hide her anger, and made a beeline to where we stood. She confronted Marsha and hollered at her about leaving Roy behind. She held nothing back.

"What happened?" she asked her. "And your excuse had better be good." Her gaze was so intense, I think she was trying to see right through Marsha's skull to find the answer.

"I searched around for him, but—" Marsha looked like a puppy who'd just chewed up a shoe.

"I don't believe you," said Mother Grace.

"Well, uh…"

"He's gone, you know," said Sister Beatrice.

"Gone?" I asked.

"He followed you; he's probably still trying to find Yasgur's Farm," said Mother Grace. It would have been funny, had Roy not been in such bad shape. "Was it really too much to ask of you? Really, Marsha? What kind of human being are you? You don't care about anyone other than yourself. You're just so—just so high and mighty."

High and Mighty. That's Marsha in a nutshell.

Sister Beatrice looked shocked at Mother Superior's candor, but didn't argue the point.

Marsha's face was bright red and tears were beginning to stream down her face.

"When did he disappear?" I asked.

"About an hour after you left." She looked at Marsha and then, not realizing the profound effect her words were having on the postulant, declared, "I don't understand why you wouldn't help him. You had no right. No right at all."

I chimed in at that point. Maybe because I wasn't thinking of what it would do to Marsha, or maybe because misery loves company, and after what happened to me I wanted her to suffer, but for some reason I said, "Yeah, especially since Janis took one of the bracelets off her arm for him to have. You know how Roy is about arms."

Sister Beatrice sighed heavily, but said nothing.

Mother Grace sighed too. "That would have made all the difference. But you destroyed it for him. Now, I'm not sure we'll ever see him again. And if he doesn't come back—" She stopped herself, but we all knew what was in her mind. "Roy has had a miserable life. He's endured things you couldn't even hope to understand. How could you do this to him?"

By that time, because she couldn't control the sobbing, Marsha's breathing was labored, and I thought she was going to throw up. She looked at Sister Beatrice, then Mother Grace, then me, then Mother Grace again.

"You're right. Everything you say about me is right. It's my fault," she cried. "If he kills himself, it will be because of me. I am good for nothing. I am not worthy to be a nun." She tore off her veil and threw it to the floor. Then she dashed out of the room. Through the window we could see her running into the grassy area behind the convent.

Sister Beatrice picked up her veil and was about to chase after her, but Mother Grace stopped her.

"Let her go," she said.

"But, I—"

"Let her go."

At that point, Mother Grace turned her attention to me. I think she knew that it wasn't my idea to ditch Roy, because she didn't seem angry with me, and asked me about what happened in Austin.

"Oh, that's terrible," she exclaimed when I explained about Threadgill's being a racist place, and my great big conscience not letting me sing there. I waited for her to put a positive spin on the whole thing. I waited for her to tell me that it was the right thing to do. That I would go nowhere in life if I didn't have respect for my black culture. That I should never allow myself to be taken in by an egocentric dream like becoming a blues singer when working in a garage was a good and decent job, and I should be happy with it because it was where God wanted me to be. That God doesn't intend everyone to be a superstar like Janis Joplin and anyway, look what it's done to her.

She didn't.

She railed at Threadgill's instead.

"You don't need that place," she said. "You'll become a blues singer without Threadgill's."

"God works in mysterious ways," said Sister Beatrice. Then she added, "You're a good singer, Easy. You'll find your way." It was nice of her to care, but I could tell by the look on her face that Marsha was dominating her thoughts. And while it was comforting to hear that they believed in my singing career, I knew it was over. I knew Janis would never call me. I knew I would never become a blues singer. I knew.

I felt pretty rotten about my life, and downhearted about Roy too. I wished he was still there at the mission. He would have loved to have had Janis Joplin's bracelet.

Does nothing in this life ever work out?

Mother Grace, usually a bubbly person who seemed to have been born from the pages of one of those "I Love Life" books, wore a frown on her face. And despite the fact that she blamed Marsha, and not me, I was aware of the role I played in Roy's disappearance. I was in such a big rush to get to Austin that I didn't insist on finding him. I could have overridden Marsha. I could have forced her to let Roy come with us. Then Roy would have had the bracelet, and would still have been at the convent getting the help he needed.

God, I wish there was something I could do. Some way of making up for what I did.

Then I remembered the bus!

"I'll be leaving for Saskatoon early tomorrow," I told the Reverend Mother, "but I have time right now, so I'd like to repair the school bus for you. Did you get those parts?"

Mother Grace pointed to a shed. "We had some things come in this morning as donations. I hope they're okay. I hope they'll fit."

"I'll make them fit." I headed for the door, then stopped and turned around. "I truly am sorry about Roy. If I'd known it was going to end up this way, I wouldn't have left without him."

Sister Beatrice and Mother Grace both nodded as I ventured outside and over to the school bus. It was a hunk of junk, to be sure, but I made it *my* mission to get it to work.

The used parts included spark plugs and an ignition coil that fit the bill, and I was able to drain the crank case and change the oil. That was enough to keep the bus running temporarily, but it needed a radiator, and that would be expensive and hard to find. I located a jug of coolant in the shed, so I flushed out the old rad as best I could and hoped it would keep things going for a while. At least until baseball season was over.

While I worked on the engine, I thought about Janis and wondered why with such amazing talent, she'd let herself be controlled by drugs and alcohol. I wasn't judging her the way Marsha did—just mulling over the reasons for it. Was it her meteoric rise to the top? Or was she influenced by being around so many people in Los Angeles who lived that kind of a life? Bessie Smith and Billie Holiday had the same issues. Maybe it was all part and parcel of being a blues singer.

Maybe it was better not to be a blues singer.

At least I'd live a longer life. Sad, boring, miserable—but long.

Oh well, I told myself. *I have my work in the garage. I like classic cars, and I can still find one to fix up for myself. Something like Johnny Foster's.*

I thought about asking Agnes if she'd let me buy it from her, but imagined she'd rather keep it close by.

I wonder why she has that photo of Wendy Wood?

Johnny must have liked her.

But why would he? I asked myself. *She was pregnant with me at the time—pregnant with a married man's child. I guess Johnny thought a lot of Clarence. Clarence certainly thought a lot of him—Johnny saved his life. He owed him everything.*

He'd do anything for Johnny. Anything.

That's Clarence, all right. He'll do anything for people he loves. That's why he took the blame for me at The Beehive.

That's why he took the blame...

I was working on the last plug when everything fell into place. Everyone and everything. I don't know why I'd repressed the questions I had about my life for so long, but my thoughts, like a car skidding toward the railing of a bridge, veered inescapably to Clarence and Wendy and Johnny. And my whole life flashed before my eyes.

CHAPTER NINETEEN

I didn't wait until the next day. I left for the airport immediately, grabbing my belongings and counting on a last-minute flight to Saskatoon. There was no time for niceties and no time for good-byes; I called a cab and headed out the door.

I passed Marsha on my way to the road; she was still crying, but I didn't give a damn. I had my own life to contend with, and wasn't about to try and console her.

"I'm leaving," I told her.

She didn't even look at me.

I was glad she was ashamed of herself, and told her so. "Your problem, Marsha, is that you judge people. Everyone you meet. Even people you *haven't* met." I glanced at the road to see if the cab was there. It wasn't, so I had time for another jab. "Remember what the Bible says, Marsha," I added. "Judge not, lest ye be judged."

She buried her face in her hands and bawled like a baby.

"I know what I've done," she mumbled, barely able to get out the words. She threw out bits of sentences, in between great big gulps of air. "I know…what I've…Now, it's…He's going to die. I did it….You don't know…what my life's…No one cares. So why—"

Half of her words were slurred. She was worse than Janis. I couldn't decipher all of what she was trying to say to me, but gathered that she'd had some kind of realization, some kind of epiphany.

I guess you could say that we'd both seen the light.

♪

It was after midnight when I crashed through the door. Clarence was sitting on the porch, trying to escape the heat of the apartment. He stirred when he heard me come in, but said nothing.

He knew what was about to come down.

When Clarence turned around and his eyes caught mine, I realized that everything I'd suspected—it was all true.

"Why didn't you tell me?"

"I did it for Thelma, Easy."

I banged my fist into the middle of the kitchen table. "Why didn't you tell me, damn it?"

"Thelma wanted a child more than anything in the world. She loved you so much. Don't you understand that you were *everything* to that woman? Absolutely *everything.*"

"How could you have done this to me?" I banged my fist again. "Let me live with a lie all these years?"

Clarence stood up and came inside. The screen door creaked when he closed it behind him. He tried to put his hand on my shoulder, but I pulled away.

"You're half white, Easy. No way anybody was going to let Thelma and me adopt a white child."

"So you said that you were my father. So Thelma could keep me."

"I had no choice."

"I can see why Wendy Wood wouldn't give a damn. You could have drowned me at birth, she wouldn't care."

"Now, Easy..."

"But what about Johnny Foster? Why was he so eager to adopt me out? What about him?"

"Johnny was a very sick man and he knew it." Clarence pulled out a chair and sat at the table. He started to push the salt and pepper shakers around like they were chess pieces— like he was figuring out his next move. "Johnny would have loved nothing more than to take you back to Amarillo with him."

"Why didn't he then?"

"Johnny had only a couple years to live, Easy. He couldn't be there for you. Not in the long run."

"What about Agnes?" I asked the question, but I knew the answer already; neither Clarence nor Thelma—and maybe not even Johnny—would want me growing up in the curio shop on Highway 66.

"Agnes is a great lady, but she couldn't be a mother to you, Easy. Not the way Thelma could."

I saw tears form in his eyes.

"I did what I had to do, Easy," he said. Then he said it again. "I did what I had to do."

I knew that. It felt like a stabbing pain in my stomach—as if the lies that had been told to me had congealed and formed a stick that was being rammed into my abdomen. But I understood why he did what he did. I loved Thelma, too. I would have done anything for her.

I sat down beside him.

"So you adopted me for Thelma's sake?"

Clarence nodded.

"And to be there for Johnny since he saved your life?"

He nodded again.

"And you were willing to take the blame all these years and put up with everyone talking about you behind your back and whispering things about you—so that you could help Johnny and give Thelma a baby?"

He paused for a long time before he replied.

"And for myself, Easy. I did it for myself. Because I loved you very much." He took my hand. "And I still do."

"But why didn't you tell me? You and Thelma should have told me, Clarence."

"We wanted to."

"Then why didn't you?" I asked.

"The time was never right," he said. "We kept putting it off, and then—"

"Thelma died."

"Yes, she died." His eyes were soft and sad.

"And?"

"Well...you despised Wendy Wood so much, Easy, that I guess I was afraid that once you knew the truth, you'd wind up hating me too." He took a handkerchief from his pocket and wiped his forehead dry. "You judge people so harshly, Easy."

"I do?"

Me? Judge people? No, that's Marsha's department.

And while I'd managed to erase his remark from my mind temporarily, I soon discovered that the accusations I'd hurled at Marsha were really about myself.

♫

Because Mrs. Hill's network of spies included the cab driver who drove me home from the airport, by Sunday at noon everyone knew I was back, so when Larry came by the garage to feed Gillie, I couldn't pretend I wasn't there. I wanted to, though. I was in no mood to talk with anybody, and preferred to stay in my room, but Larry called and called through the door, and he wasn't going away.

"Easy!" he shouted from outside the garage. "Easy, are you up yet?" With that much noise, I don't know why he bothered to ask. "Easy!" he hollered again.

Because it was Sunday, and we were closed, I went around the back and let him in the side door.

"Hi," I said, in the voice I normally reserved for proselytizing Jehovah's Witnesses. He looked so happy, I felt I had to add "How are you?" I didn't really care one way or another.

He gave me a big bear hug. My arms dangled beside me

while he squeezed me like an orange. "I'm great," he said. "I want to hear about your trip." Realizing it would be better to deal with him and get the conversation out of the way, I pulled a couple of sodas out of the cooler, and we went outside and sat on the tailgate of a pickup truck.

"Thanks," he said, when I gave him the pop. He shoved an envelope into his pocket.

"What's that?" I asked.

"A letter home to my brother," he replied. "With a check inside." He took a swig of soda. "I'm heading to the mailbox next."

"A check?"

"It's my folks' anniversary and we're all chipping in to buy them a gift."

"That's nice," I said, envisioning my future with nothing in it but motor oil and chitchat about Porcupine Plain.

"I didn't know if I'd have enough money saved in time," admitted Larry, "and that had me feeling lower than a fat frog in a dry well." He tipped up the pop bottle, then clunked it down so dramatically, you'd think it was a mickey of rye and he'd just returned from the Alamo. "But I've been cuttin' it close to the bone, and managed to put twenty dollars away."

"What are you getting them?" I asked.

"A septic tank."

I choked on my drink. "A septic tank? Well...uh...I hope they're happy with it."

"They will be," he said with a smile. "So tell me about your trip to the desert."

"Didn't you get my postcard?" I asked. "Actually, I've got another one that I never mailed. You can have that one, too."

"I didn't get a postcard, at least not yet." He was clearly disappointed. "Maybe it'll be here tomorrow."

"Too late to be bothered with it."

"No it isn't," he declared. "I love postcards. My brother sent me one from Niagara Falls when he got married."

Oh, no. He's on to weddings. Now he's going to tell me about the one I missed.

"Well, Larry," I said, glancing at my wrist where there was no watch, "I'd better be getting back inside. I've got a ton of laundry to do."

"Please stay another minute," he begged. "I want to hear about your trip. What was it like in the good ol' *Yew S of A*?"

I gave him a quick summary of the events, hoping it would satisfy him and I could get on my way.

"Gee, I'm real sorry that it didn't work out with Janis Joplin," he said.

"Yeah," I replied, looking at his pop bottle to see how much was left in order to calculate how much time I'd have to sit there. It wasn't that I didn't like Larry, but at that abysmally low point in my life, I was feeling sorry for myself and didn't have the energy for anyone.

That was when Larry hijacked the conversation and swung it around to Skeeter.

"You missed a fabulous wedding, you know. It was really nice."

192

Yeah, I'll bet it was. He probably spent the whole night in the stag line with a bunch of hunched-over fifteen-year-old boys.

"My brother and Skeeter were real upset that you couldn't make it. They were looking forward to meeting you."

"Yeah, well—look, I've got a lot to do today, Larry."

I jumped off the back of the truck and was ready to go inside and sulk, but Larry hadn't finished all of what he wanted to say.

"I played the tape of you singing. I played it for Skeeter and a good friend of hers. I met him at the wedding—great guy. His father—"

"You did what?" I hollered. "I didn't give you permission to do that! I didn't want that stupid Skeeter woman to hear my tape, let alone anybody else."

"She asked me to bring it, Easy, because—"

"I don't care!"

I felt blood boiling inside my ears.

Now I didn't like Larry at all. I hated him.

What right did he have to play the tape? I didn't even want to be taped in the first place.

"But Skeeter—"

"I don't give a damn about Skeeter, or your brother, or your septic tank, or anything else about you, Larry. That was a dirty trick." Seething with rage, I started for the door.

Larry ran behind me.

"But this friend of Skeeter's, his father listened to the tape, and he wants to give you an audition, Easy. He thinks you're terrific."

I stopped.

"Audition?" My back was still turned.

"You'll probably be singing on weeknights to start, but—"

I wheeled around to face Larry.

"What the hell are you talking about?"

"He owns a place here in town."

"You're out of your mind, Larry. There are only two clubs in this town, so unless this guy is George Penn and owns The Beehive—"

"No, he doesn't own The Beehive. He has a really nice place. It's called Saskatoon Blues."

♪

I wore the green dress that Thelma made for me. The one we worked on together for my graduation. What else could I wear for my opening night at the club? At the club where Billie Holiday once sang.

I watched as Clarence took a seat. I don't know if it was thanks to the owner insisting he have the best table in the place, or if it was thanks to Mrs. Hill for making sure everyone in Saskatoon knew the truth about him, but it was the first time my father felt comfortable enough to sit at the front. And in his brand new suit, he sure looked like *Mister* Merritt.

To his left was Larry, that big white toothy grin of his lighting up more of the table than the candle in the centerpiece. I figured his mother must have made a one-time exception and let him get within a hundred paces of alcohol. It was hard to believe that it was thanks to a guy from Porcupine Plain and a woman named Skeeter that I finally had a chance at a career as a blues singer.

Clarence found an empty chair and pulled it next to him at the table.

I knew that one was for Thelma.

I picked up the microphone.

"I'd like to dedicate my first song to my parents, Thelma and Clarence Merritt," I said, and Clarence wiped his eyes with the back of his hand.

It was "God Bless the Child," and when I sang it to that empty chair, it wasn't empty anymore.

CHAPTER TWENTY

October 5, 1970
It was on a Monday afternoon that I heard the news about Janis. I was alone at the time—Clarence and Larry had gone to Regina for parts—and I'd been thinking about her a lot. Wondering if I'd ever see her again, yet somehow knowing that I never would.

I just hadn't figured on the reason.

Then I turned on the radio:

Rock Star Janis Joplin is dead at the age of twenty-seven. Known for her full-throttle performances and uninhibited lifestyle, the blues singer was found yesterday in her room at the Landmark Motor Hotel in Los Angeles, dead of an apparent overdose of heroin.

The announcer went on to say that Janis and her band had been working on an album for the past month at the Sunset Sound Recording Studio. When he said it—in a voice that was distant and cold—I wondered how the life of someone so free-spirited, so incomparable, could be reduced to a twenty-second news item. At that time, of course, I had no way of knowing that "Me and Bobby McGee" would hit number one on the charts.

That's her legacy. Not the crap people say about her.

It's hard to explain how Janis's death affected me. It was a different kind of pain than I felt after losing Thelma—that kind cuts right through you and leaves a rift in your heart that never heals. Never.

With Janis, I felt anger. Anger at the stupidity of a twenty-seven-year-old woman with the best voice on the planet throwing her life away to drugs and alcohol. And while looking at things in retrospect ordinarily blunts corners, the passing of time has never made me feel any different.

Just like the black blues singers she venerated, her life had been one of turmoil. I couldn't help but wonder if fate had played a hand—October 4th was the same day Bessie Smith was buried in 1937. And Janis had put a headstone on her grave just a few weeks before her own death.

When Marsha roared through our lot in the yellow submarine, I knew exactly why she'd come. I pushed up the garage door and went out to meet her.

The driver's side door swung open and out she slid. I hadn't seen her since that evening in July when I left her in Albuquerque, crying over what she'd done to Roy.

"So you heard?" I asked her.

"Late last night," she said. "Sister Beatrice and I were almost back to Saskatoon when it came over the radio. It's—it's horrible."

"I didn't think you cared much for Janis," I remarked.

"I hated her, you know that."

"And you don't anymore?"

"After what happened with Roy, I learned…well, I learned not to hate anyone. Let's just say I learned what hate can do. And it frightened me."

"It did?"

"After you left," she told me, "I worked every day in the mission. Mother Grace forgave me, and I went to confession more than I ever have in my life. The priest helped me work through a lot of things."

"So…um…did Roy ever—"

"No. He didn't come back." Her eyes hit the ground.

"I'm sorry to hear that. I hope the news about Janis doesn't make him do anything foolish."

"I hope he's still—"

"Alive?" I asked, and Marsha nodded.

I sighed and leaned on the hood of the car. "If he is out there someplace, he'll make his way back to Mother Grace. She's a magnet."

Like Janis. She was a magnet, too.

As I thought about Janis, I glanced at Marsha's wrist and wondered about the gold bangle.

"The bracelet—"

"Mother Grace is keeping it for Roy. In case he comes back," she said.

We were both quiet for a long time, then she looked at me closely. "I'm sorry for you, Easy, because I know you thought so much of Janis."

Her remark was like a plug, that when pulled, made everything gush.

"I can't stand the thought of her dying like that. All alone in some lousy hotel room. All alone! Janis Joplin!" I shook my head. "I wish now that I had tried to help her in some way. Not that I could do much. But I was so impressed by her, so in awe of her, that I didn't even think about her heroin abuse. I didn't think anything could bring her down. If it had been anyone else, I would have tried to intervene. And now it's too late."

"It's hard to live with regrets," said Marsha.

"It is."

We were quiet again, and I began to think about something else I regretted.

"I'm sorry for what I said in Albuquerque—when I accused you of judging people."

"You were right. The things I said about Janis Joplin were horrible and hateful. She treated me with respect, and I gave her none in return."

I didn't know how to reply, so I changed the subject and asked about her plans.

"I'll be receiving my full habit in a few days," she said. "Then I'm on my way to Alberta."

"Would you do something for me, Marsha? When you're in Calgary?"

"If I can."

"I've been saving money for some time now—to buy a car. But do you remember that 1951 Chevy—behind the curio shop in Amarillo?"

"Yeah, I think so."

"I've kept in touch with Agnes Foster over the last few months, and Clarence and I are going down to visit her. Larry's going to look after the garage while we're gone."

"Larry?"

"He's our apprentice," I explained. "And a good friend." I smiled. "Anyway, Clarence wants to see Route 66 again—you know, before it's gone. And I'd like to see more of it myself."

"Right," said Marsha.

"Well, I'm pretty sure Agnes is going to let me have the car—I'm going to restore it to its original condition. So I've got several hundred dollars that I won't be needing now, and—"

"But what has that got to do with me?"

"There's a woman in Calgary. She's homeless and known to frequent the mission downtown—in the East Village. I doubt you'd have much trouble finding her. Her name is Wendy Wood and, well—"

Marsha took a pad out of her purse and wrote down the name. "Wendy Wood," she mumbled.

"She used to be a good singer, but she needs a lot of dental work. I have enough to cover it, if you wouldn't mind helping her to find a dentist."

"Well—sure I will, but—"

"You can't just hand her the money. She might—"

"Spend it on something else," said Marsha.

"Right. I'd like her to be able to sing."

"Okay…well, I'll do my best."

"Thanks."

We stood there for a minute, then I offered Marsha a soda. She declined. (Still the same Marsha in many ways, she said anything carbonated goes up the back of her nose.) Then I asked about her new name. "What's it going to be? Sister Bohuslava or Sister Nastasiya?" I could only recall two of her choices—but I knew they had to do with God's grace and the resurrection. Something religious like that.

"Neither of those," she said.

"Oh," I replied. "You picked something different?"

"Yes, Easy, I have," she said, and by the look on her face I could tell it was special. "I realized this morning that it was the only one that would ever be right," continued Marsha. "I wasn't sure whether or not the Mother Superior would approve it, but when I told her why I had chosen that name—why I wanted to carry it with me for the rest of my life, to remind myself never to be high and mighty again—she gave me her full blessing."

Then it hit me.

"Oh, my God," I said. "You're going to be Sister Janis?"

"No," said Marsha, "not Sister Janis." She looked up to the sky, like she was trying to see through the clouds, and then she turned to me. "I'm going to be Sister Pearl."

THE FESTIVAL EXPRESS

In the summer of 1970, a fourteen-car passenger train, its baggage car painted with giant orange letters reading "Festival Express," pulled out of Toronto carrying some of the era's most fabled musicians. The infamous boozy five-day train trip halted in Calgary and Winnipeg to give legendary performances by The Grateful Dead, The Band, Sha Na Na, Ian and Sylvia, and many more. Joplin, who by all accounts was the presiding life of the party, stole the show, of course, although her penchant for Southern Comfort and heroin had already begun to take its toll, as revealed in film footage from the Calgary gig, where the singer stumbles more than once, but still mesmerizes everyone in the venue.

Known as Canada's Woodstock, the trip—including the stop at Saskatoon to buy out a trackside liquor store—was recorded on film and has since become the subject of a remarkable documentary, due to the fact that some of the hottest music was played on the train itself. Sadly, the performances at Toronto, Winnipeg, and Calgary would be some of Joplin's last. She died only three months later.

ACKNOWLEDGMENTS

The research and writing of this novel benefitted by funding from an Ontario Arts Council Writers' Reserve grant.

Many thanks to Margie, Kathryn, Carolyn and everyone at Second Story Press for their ongoing support of my work. The encouragement that I have received from these hardworking and insightful women has made all the difference in both my professional and personal life.

ABOUT THE AUTHOR

CAROLINE STELLINGS is an award-winning author and illustrator of numerous books for children and young adults, including *The Contest* and the Nicki Haddon Mystery Series. She has been nominated for many prizes and has won both the ForeWord Book of the Year and the Hamilton Literary Award for Fiction. She lives in Waterdown, Ontario.